Mystery of the Golden Shells

An Adventure Story

Jennifer M Zeiger

Illustrated

by

Justin Allen

Published by Jennifer M Zeiger of Zeiger Adventure Publishing

Edited by Darren Thornberry

Printed by IngramSpark

First Edition: August 15, 2022

Cover Design and Illustrations by Justin Allen

ISBN 978-1-7351226-4-9

jenniferzeiger.com
jennifer.m.zeiger@gmail.com

Mom and Dad
For never doubting

<u>Attention</u>

This book is not intended for you to read straight through! Heaven knows, it'll make no sense if you do.

Instead, read until the book gives you a choice on what to do and then follow the directions to see what happens. Some decisions will lead to success and friendships, and others, my poor reader, may lead to misfortune or even death.

Choose wisely for there be dangerous men and beasts within these seemingly innocent pages.

Best of luck!

Capital City draws every kind of trade from powerful horses to lush fruits to rare, magic-crafted jewelry made to warm the wearer and keep her dry in the heavy spring rains. With such diverse commerce, the markets seethe and flow with people, making your skin crawl at the close press of the crowds.

You don't often travel into the city from your beloved Alder forest. For a moment, you imagine you're hunting an angry troll for the King. As you hunt, you're surrounded by the tangy smell of pine and the cold bite of mountain wind, but then the odor of sweat and heat smothers the fantasy and you're back in the chatter of the crowds. You'd rather face the troll than listen to the yell of the street vendors.

But then a familiar call catches your ear and you smile. When you do brave the salt brine of the city, you make it a point to stop by the fruit vendor who sets up his stand along the wharf. He sells tangy mangos brought in from the south, sweet strawberries, and salty, fried plantains. You order a ripe mango and, while you savor the fruit, the noise of the docks fades into the bellowing of beasts.

It's while you're enjoying this small reprieve with the fruit's juices coating your fingers that an older man taps your shoulder.

"Spare a piece of mango?" he asks.

"Of course." And you slice off a chunk with your knife.

As he takes it, he asks, "Spare an arm to help me down the road?"

"Go away, old man," the fruit vendor scolds him. "You're bothering my customer."

"It's no bother," you say, tucking your knife into the sheath in the top of your boot before offering your arm to the old man.

Together, you wander down the crowded street with the call of other vendors carrying after you and the odor of roasting meat clinging to the air. A lanky man stumbles, bumping your shoulder and, out of reflex, your fingers tense on the mango in your free hand. Immediately, juices start to drip through your fingers.

The old man's grip tightens on your arm and he directs you around a corner heading toward the docks. Once you're away from the market, he steps back to straighten his bent posture and adjust his tattered jacket.

You give him a small bow, saying, "Greetings, Robert." This is the King's steward—the Hand, for short—and your employer.

He smooths his white hair and grins. "Play a pretty good old codger, don't I?" But then his smile fades. "I'm glad you're in your usual outfit or I might never have realized you're in the city." He refers to your unique, multi-pocketed pants and supple leather jacket. "Got your supplies?" he asks.

"All but my weapons." You left your longbow and cutlass behind, knowing they'd make the citizens of the capital nervous. But you do have your water, hidden away in the pocket against your left thigh, and your jerky rations, in the pocket above your right knee.

"Good. I've got work for you."

"What beast's causing trouble now?" You pull out your knife again to finish your mango but your brain is already running through the usual spring beasts: bears, trolls, some cats…

"A poisonous one."

"A snake?"

"A man…or possibly a woman."

You pause with a mango slice midway to your mouth, wondering if he's gone crazy, but he seems sane enough. You eat the bite and admit, "I don't deal well with people."

"I know," he winces apologetically, "but you're the only hunter the palace doesn't recognize on sight."

A poisonous person, the palace, and a hunter people don't recognize. "Someone poisoned the King," you conclude.

"The Queen," Robert clarifies.

"What are the job details?"

He gestures for you to walk with him again. You offer him the last of your fruit but he shakes his head while he explains, "We've set up a 'contest' on Isbell Island. Whoever's the first to find a golden shell wins the whole island." He directs your steps down the docks.

"Aren't there three golden shells?" you ask, being somewhat familiar with the stories.

"According to myth, but no one's ever found them."

You lick the mango juice off your fingers while you think. The contest idea makes sense as the King regularly offers such challenges, rewarding the winners with land, and it won't raise suspicions.

But why Isbell Island?

"Isn't Isbell a place of wild magic and dangerous beasts?" you ask.

"Yes. It has everything from portals to transformation magic, but supposedly the golden shells are magically healing as well."

The terrible mix of wild unknowns makes you shudder. "Is the Queen that ill?"

"She is."

You bow your head. The King must be desperate to resort to mythical healing shells.

"The other contestants are the suspects we've been able to narrow it down to," Robert continues. "Your task will be to search for a shell and figure out who poisoned our Queen."

"The suspects?"

"A performer, a storyteller, a scribe, a cook, and a manservant who's the King's dresser. They all work in the palace and have been slighted by the Queen recently." Robert stops you with a hand. "You only have a few days, Hunter. Here," he hands over a golden medallion bearing the King's coat of arms. You recognize it as a justice badge, granting you authority to apprehend the poisoner.

You slip the medallion's strap over your head and tuck it below your shirt while Robert gestures toward a ship called the *King's Justice.*

Fitting, you think.

"The other contestants are already aboard," Robert says. "Good luck."

As you head down the pier, you suddenly wish you'd brought your weapons. You sigh. You'll just have to content yourself with your knife and your wits.

Once on the ship, the crew directs you below deck while they cast off. You lower yourself down the companionway, being careful not to let your land legs trip you as the ship sways.

At the thud of your boots, a scrawny old man pops his head above the counter in the galley. He shoves a hand through his steel-gray hair and exclaims, "Jumping jugglers, another contestant!"

Since it's not a question, you don't respond.

He continues without noticing. "No matter. Mark my promise, Allen will win no matter how many contestants the King includes."

He stands up holding three late-season mandarins, which he starts juggling, sending the fruits toward the beams above in a high arch. As he passes by, his long coat flutters, revealing the red, yellow, and green patches on his pants that cover gallon-deep pockets.

There's a snort and you look back to find a dark haired gypsy woman scowling at the old man. She sips from a glass in her bejeweled fingers that gives off the faint whiff of rum. "Performing parrot, he always talks about himself in the third person. It's disgraceful," she says.

"Allen heard that," hollers the old man.

"Patricia doesn't care!" responds the woman.

Suddenly, a mandarin sails out of the darkness from the other end of the ship.

Patricia fumbles, sloshing her rum, but catches the fruit. She scowls even harder and crow's feet fan out from the corners of her dark eyes.

You hear a telltale *whoosh* and another mandarin comes sailing your way. Snagging it, you drop it into a pocket for later.

Patricia peels her mandarin like she wanted it in the first place, dropping the slices into her drink.

"Storytelling is far more refined than what that trickster does," she says.

Then, taking your raised brow as agreement, she wanders away.

The ship creaks, heeling to starboard. Above, sailors shout and there's the snap of sails catching the wind, but for the moment you're alone and you take stock.

Patricia's the storyteller and Allen's the performer. Where are the cook, scribe, and dresser?

The galley and saloon are obviously empty and it'd be awkward to go searching for them, so instead you start rummaging in the galley, hoping to find more fruit. With delight, you spot three fresh oranges and a bag of figs. Tucking your treasures away, you sit down and wait.

While you do, you take in the barrels of water strapped to the hull and the two racks of weapons bolted near the companionway. They're full of swords and bows, the crew's

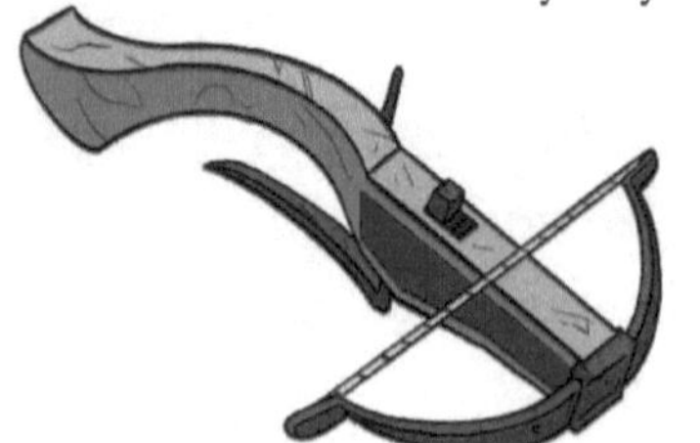

weapons, but there's one conspicuously empty slot that appears right for a small crossbow.

"Land ahoy!" a sailor shouts above. "Longboat's hittin' water for the contestants."

You climb on deck to find Patricia standing beside a towering young man in a green doublet. His long fingers separate the slices of a mandarin before he carefully eats one piece at a time. Suddenly, Patricia snatches his last two slices and eats them, cackling at his cat-like look of shock.

When you step up beside them at the rail, he glances over and points at your boots. "Nice leather. Needs polishing."

"Leave it alone, Marius Jack," Patricia scolds, her humor vanishing. "Not everyone wants their clothes stiff and shiny."

So, this is the dresser, you think while he smooths his collar and ducks his suddenly red cheeks.

A moment later, Allen distracts them by hopping on deck and skipping to the rail.

He's so lively that you almost miss the man who stumbles out of the companionway behind him. The man catches himself on the wall while clutching a small leatherbound book with his free hand. His fingers are stained around the nails with a deep blue ink. Straightening himself, he scurries over, reminding you of a ferret hurrying away with its treasures.

Finally, the last member of the group emerges, blinking her bright green eyes in the brilliant sunlight. Absently, she brushes at her hair, which frames her face in a feathery cloud of owl-white fluff, and moves to join the ferret-like man.

The scribe and cook, you figure.

Everyone's loaded into the longboat and rowed to shore before you get the chance to be properly introduced.

"We'll be anchored in the bay," a sailor says. "The Hand's going to join us soon. First one to find a shell, come wave us in."

Then, as the longboat rows away, Allen exclaims, "Show's started! See you lollygaggers later." And the performer skips off into the trees.

As he does, you catch a glimpse of the thatched roof of a hut through the palms farther inland, but a glance around shows you no one else has seen it yet.

You don't mention it as the others look at each other. Then, like there's an unspoken cue, they all disperse without a word. The cook follows at the scribe's heels while the dresser and the storyteller go their own ways.

Your first inclination is to follow one of them to start investigating which one's the poisoner, but with your twofold mission, you pause and the hut draws your attention again. It seems obvious, but it might be just the place to hide a shell. Do you follow someone or go search the hut?

____

To search the hut, go to page 19
To follow someone, go to page 25

After everyone has left, the island sits silent beyond the low thud of the waves crashing on the sand. Some other sense tickles your nerve endings like a feather over your neck. *Magic.* The island practically breathes with it in every gust of wind.

You scan the cove.

The sand is off-white and gray with shells, seaweed, and driftwood peeking through. At the far edge of the beach, tall grasses sway where they grow on top of the dunes, and beyond them you spot a mix of palms, southern magnolias, and pines. Breathing in deep, you catch the sweet scent of the white blossoms growing on the trees.

As you take the island's atmosphere in, warblers start trilling their high, sharp song and you take their chatter as your cue to search the hut now that everyone's moved on.

You find a bamboo structure with four simple walls. It feels peaceful with its clean thatched roof shading the steps leading inside and the glassless windows letting in patches of soft sunlight. Your boots thud on the floor as you move past the square table to run a palm across the bar. To the left, a vague painting of a sparkling waterfall hangs, and you pause to study it.

As you reach to pull the painting free, the

warblers outside go silent again. Cautiously, you grab for your knife.

"Burning rings!" Allen, the performer, bursts through the door. "You beat me to it."

You drop your knife back into your boot before he notices the weapon. And then you turn again to pull the painting off the wall.

"Say now, what're you doing?"

Usually, you'd ignore such an obvious question but you haven't forgotten Robert's other order. *Figure out who poisoned the Queen.*

"You perform for the King and Queen?" you ask, ignoring his question while you flip the painting over to inspect the back. There's nothing but a wire with which to hang the painting and a couple metal screws.

Seeing what you're doing, Allen taps the side of his thin nose and pulls another painting off the adjacent wall. You catch a glimpse of a cave with a lake inside before he flips it over.

"Allen gave them some of the best performances they'd ever seen," he answers in third person again, "but her Ladyship complained anyway." He smacks the frame of his painting onto the bar with a sharp crack.

You jerk, more out of surprise at the action than the sound, but Allen grins and eyes you like a monkey right before it jumps.

You turn away, ignoring him, to rehang

your painting and he chuckles.

"And what did they do to poor Allen?" he continues with his story. "They tossed him to the cobblestones."

You miss the hook for the painting and try again while he grumbles. Suddenly, he shifts topics, "But this contest! It'll fix everything so long as the others don't muck it up." He pauses and then observes, "You know, I kind of recognize the others. Not by name, mind you, but at least by face. But not you. What part of the palace do you work in again?"

Finally, you catch the painting's hook but you tug harder on it than intended. A faint click sounds and something shifts beneath your feet.

A trapdoor?

You step away quickly and glance at Allen. He's tugging at the frame of his painting in an effort to pull it apart. Before he notices your hesitation, you move toward the third and last picture that hangs by the doorway. As you do, something catches your attention over Allen's shoulder.

"Hold up," you say, stopping him from ripping the canvas out of its frame. He scowls but stops.

Didn't want me to see it, you realize.

Suddenly, he holds out a mandarin that he must have pulled from a pocket. "Fruit?"

What's with the mandarins? You're not sure but you shake your head and answer, "Still have one from earlier."

"That's good then," he says and the mandarin disappears back into a green-patched pocket. Then, as an afterthought, he pulls it back out and begins to peel the thick rind away, filling the hut with the sweet, strong citrus scent of an overripe fruit.

"Pretty angry with the Queen," you mutter while you study the drawing.

"Bet your balance I am!" he says around a slice of mandarin. "Can't get hired when the Queen's smirched your reputation."

Although the drawing looks like a child's pencil sketch, it clearly has the outline of the island and several distinctive similarities to the paintings around the hut. "This must be the cove we got dropped off in, and that looks like the hut," you say, pointing.

Allen's eyes drop to the canvas and a grin grows across his face, the monkey similarity returning. "This here's got to be a cave or something, and this…err…maybe another cove?"

It's a cliff with a waterfall, but you don't point out its similarities to the painting you just rehung.

"Three shells, three locations!" Allen starts hopping from one foot to the other. "This hut's probably been searched clean, don't ya think, but these other two spots…let's check this one." And his finger lands on the cliffs. Then he spins and heads for the door.

His shift in focus catches you by surprise and he's out the door before you can answer.

His motive for poisoning is pretty strong and staying with him might reveal if he's simply a disgruntled old performer or if he actually poisoned the Queen.

But there's also the latch you felt release in the floor. You suspect it's a trapdoor and if you stay, you can investigate it along with the rest of the hut.

To go with Allen, go to page 89
To investigate the hut's floor, go to page 117

After everyone has left, the island sits silent beyond the low thud of the waves crashing on the sand. Some other sense tickles your nerve endings like a feather over your neck. *Magic.* The island practically breathes with it in every gust of wind.

You scan the cove.

The sand is off-white and gray with shells, seaweed, and driftwood peeking through the grains. At the far edge of the beach, tall grasses sway where they grow on top of the dunes, and beyond them you spot a mix of palms, southern magnolias, and pines. Breathing in deep, you catch the sweet scent of the white blossoms growing on the trees.

As you take the island's atmosphere in, warblers start trilling their high, sharp song and you take their chatter as your cue to start following someone.

Continue on page 27

By the time you move to follow someone, the other contestants are nowhere in sight, but their passage pressed wide trails in the tall grass over the dunes. This doesn't surprise you as you've found most humans leave trails as wide as a troll's. Soon enough, you find a magnolia with its glossy leaves broken and it becomes a simple matter to follow the scuffed earth and disturbed foliage left by two sets of feet.

The sandy loam squishes beneath your boots while a soft breeze carries the ocean's briny scent from the waves. As the wind brushes your skin, your nerves tingle and you shudder. Never before have you experienced a place so saturated with wild magic. The feel of it continues to tease your nerves even as you move inland.

It's not long before you overhear two voices ahead and you peer through the thick branches of an magnolia to spot the scribe and the cook.

"Will the King actually award either of us the island?" the cook asks in soprano tones surprisingly similar to a wren's.

"His Hand said he would. I've never heard him lie," answers the scribe. You again think of a ferret with how his long frame hunches over and his head hangs, staring at the ground like the rodent standing on its feet.

They meander along, lacking the purposeful gait you're used to from hiking the forest. You lean against the stalky trunk of a palm and wait.

Again, the wind brushes your skin and your nerves tighten, but when you glance at the two walking ahead, they continue to meander in a comfortable stroll.

Perhaps they don't feel the brush of magic. It wouldn't be the first time you've encountered people who are unaware of its touch.

A long stretch of quiet follows and you glance to make sure they're still walking.

They are and you creep forward, past the palm and behind the scraggly branches of a fallen oak, before you settle again to let them gain distance on you.

Such comfortable silence between two individuals speaks of long acquaintance, you figure.

Suddenly, the girl says, "Wish I'd had a chance to explain to the Queen 'bout my mistake. I didn't realize she was allergic to shellfish."

"She'll come around," the scribe answers, clearly familiar with the topic.

You sit on the dead oak, gauging their

conversation in light of the Queen's poisoning. If the cook had wanted to kill the Queen, she clearly could have done it already as the shellfish incident indicates. So, either she miscalculated on the amount of shellfish, or she bears no ill will against the Queen.

You're still not sure about the scribe. He seems protective of the cook and you wonder if he'd be willing to poison someone to protect her.

You get off the log and follow, noticing their voices have grown faint. The sandy loam keeps your steps silent but you still tread lightly, not wanting to get careless.

"Uncle Nessen," the girl continues a while later. "Do you think we have a chance at finding a shell?"

Uncle? Well, that explains their comfortable camaraderie and the scribe's protectiveness.

The scribe chuckles and you hear him tap the book he was clutching on the ship. "Don't fret, Mia," he says. "I might just have a riddle to help us out."

Your ears perk up at that, and then a warning prickle travels your spine. It's not the nerve-tingling sensation caused by magic, but something else altogether. You go still, listening to the island's sounds.

Ahead, Nessen, the scribe, opens his book and leans in to share with Mia what it says, but you listen beyond that.

There's the trickle of a nearby river and the chittering of a squirrel, but neither of these caused the spine-tingling warning. Suddenly, the squirrel goes silent mid-chatter and it's the quiet left in its wake that confirms your suspicions.

The last time such silence engulfed you was when you startled a roc—a giant bird rivaling the size of a small dragon—from its nest. Every animal nearby went utterly still, terrified of the enormous predator rising noiselessly behind you. Only the heavy wind of the bird's wings had saved you before it descended, heavy claws open to snag you.

But the most terrifying predators who like to sneak up on a person are felines. They make no sound; there's no whoosh of wings to suddenly warn of danger. And the sandy loam that makes it easy for you to stay quiet would also aid slinking paws.

Isbell Island, you realize with a sinking sensation, is the perfect place for mottled leopards. With the shifting sunlight dappling the island floor, they'd blend into smooth, stalking shadows.

You fall back even farther from the scribe and cook and pick a sturdy pine tree to climb.

Sap sticks to your palms as you haul yourself into the branches, but once you're well into the fragrant needles, you turn your back against the trunk and look around.

You spot the owl-white hair of Mia and the hunched form of Nessen. They stopped not far ahead to drink from the fast moving river you heard before. The cook even set down her small pack, settling in for a longer break.

You scan for movement, any movement, but particularly the slow, stealthy slink of a feline. There's only the sparkling of the river in the sunshine and the motion of the other two contestants.

Then something stirs the palm fronds farther up the river. It's not the slink of a predator but the jerky motion of a man falling out of the bushes at the river's edge. You recognize the green doublet of Marius Jack, the dresser, but he's no longer standing tall like he had on the ship. Instead, he crawls to the river's edge and cups a hand into the water. He gets a few sips before he pauses, fighting the shaking that's shuddering the leaves around him.

Poisoned?

Just when you think this, he hunches forward, clutching his stomach, and keels over into the river head first.

You spin and are halfway down the tree when Mia screams, which is immediately followed by a familiar gritty roaring.

You hesitate. Marius Jack is quite possibly unconscious in the river, being carried by the current to who knows where. But Mia and Nessen are facing one of the very predators from which you're supposed to protect people.

To help Marius Jack, go to page 35
To help Mia and Nessen, go to page 63

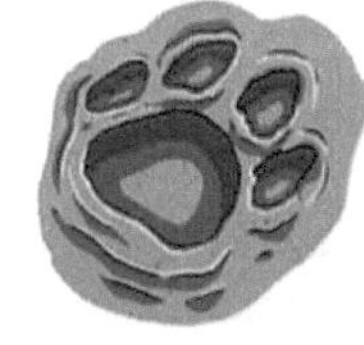

Choosing to either save Marius Jack from the rushing river or protect Mia and Nessen from an attacking leopard might be one of the hardest decisions of your life. Mia's scream makes your insides ache but you finally decide she has her uncle to help her whereas Marius Jack can't even help himself.

Before you drop out of the pine, you place him again where he's floating in the river. Even in the seconds since you spotted him, he's washed dozens of feet downstream. Knowing the current will continue to carry him before you reach the river, you drop from the pine and tear off through the trees.

Moments later, you burst out onto the riverbank, frantically searching for the familiar green doublet of the dresser.

There!

Marius Jack floats face up but limp on the far side of the flowing stream. He hangs up briefly on a rock before getting pulled into the current again.

You wade in, expecting the cold bite of snow-fed water like you're used to in the Alder forest. Instead, the river's warm and doesn't steal your breath when you dive in.

Swimming hard, you reach for Marius Jack's doublet, miss, reach again, and snag your fingers in the sodden velvet. With one arm, you haul Marius Jack against your torso and with the other you paddle for the shore, gasping as water splashes your face and sneaks into your mouth.

Only a little farther! You fix your eyes on the riverbank.

Finally, your kicking legs hit sand and you shove yourself and Marius Jack out of the water. You stumble and hit your knees, wheezing for air.

After a moment, you turn to the dresser. His chest isn't moving with the rise and fall of breath. *Need him on firmer ground,* you think, and grab him under the shoulders to haul his lanky frame completely clear of the water.

He twitches and you nearly drop him. Steadying yourself, you lower him again and roll him onto his side as he twitches and heaves, coughing up water.

If he was poisoned, it could be from something he ate, you realize.

"Throw it all up," you tell him.

He gives a blurry, "Huh?" and begins to rise but coughs again.

You urge him to pivot to kneel at the water's edge, supporting his shuddering frame as you answer, "Throw up whatever you can."

Still bleary, he simply does as directed.

Then, finished, he slumps back, still sitting in the water and smacking his tongue with a "yuck" expression pinching his lips. You pull your water skin from its pocket and offer him a drink to clear his mouth.

He swishes the water, spits, swishes and spits again, and then takes a long swallow before slumping back against you to stare at the toes of his boots where they peek out of the river in front of him.

Suddenly, he stiffens and points at his feet, croaking, "It'll take hours to fix the water damage!"

"Least you're alive," you say.

He jerks and truly looks at you for the first time. A confused expression washes over his face. "I felt ill and heard the river nearby," he mutters. "Worked my way toward it. I remember getting a sip." He refocuses on you, taking in your dripping hair and clothes. "You saved me?"

Seems obvious, so you don't answer. Instead, you raise a brow.

He scrubs a hand across his face. "Did someone poison me?"

This is a better question. "Believe so," you answer. "You fell into the water."

"The other contestants are that ruthless?" he asks, but doesn't wait for an answer as he continues, "I never thought someone would try to *kill* the other contestants." He tries to straighten his collar, finds it's soaked and limp, and gives up with a weak wave.

He seems genuinely shocked. You debate for a second but finally decide to trust him.

"One of them poisoned the Queen as well. I'm here to figure out who." You show him the King's medallion and ask, "What have you eaten since boarding the ship?"

He stares at you and blinks. "Wait," he says, "the contest's not real? The shells?"

"No, they're real. They heal people. I'm searching for those too. What have you eaten?"

He frowns, brushing at the sand stuck to his doublet. It's still wet though and the sand sticks to his fingers. "Patricia poured me a glass of rum," he says, "and I ate a mandarin from the old performer as well."

Allen or Patricia then, you think. It's not conclusive, but it gives you a place to start.

But not immediately, because the sun's setting through the trees and Marius Jack has started to shiver.

"Let's get a small fire going," you say, "and get you dry."

By the time the sun's down, a small fire crackles cheerily with its light flickering on the nearby tree trunks. Near it, Marius Jack sits comfortably against a rock. You dragged him there because no matter how long he ordered his legs to move, they're not responding. The immobility further confirms that poison was involved in his dunking but he seems comfortable now, so you leave him long enough to investigate the spot where you saw Nessen and Mia downriver. All you find are scuff marks, what appears to be a shattered wooden box, and some blood but not enough to kill someone.

It's enough for now to know they got away alive.

You return to the fire and sit across from the dresser while the desire for sleep steals a yawn from you.

"Patricia or Allen," you say, returning to the question of who poisoned Marius Jack and likely the Queen.

Marius Jack gives a drowsy, "Mmhm."

"Have to return to the beach to track them," you mutter. "We'll lose half a day tomorrow and the trail will be cold."

"Maybe not," Marius Jack perks up. "They *are* playing the contest like everyone else, so they'll go to wherever the shells are supposed to be."

You eye him, admitting, "We don't know where the shells are supposed to be."

"No, but my nana always told a story about when pops was a steward here. He found a portal and, according to myth, all the portals take you to shell locations. I was searching for pops' portal when I fell into the river."

"Where's your pops' portal go?"

He shrugs. "That part of the story gets confusing. Something about a dark lake."

You pull out a piece of jerky to eat while you consider. Marius Jack is right. Patricia and Allen *will* go to wherever they think they can find a shell.

If you can find Marius Jack's portal, it might take you directly to where you need to be, but you shudder, a little hesitant to make use of something created by wild magic.

As you think about it, it occurs to you the scribe, Nessen, might also know of a shell location because of his riddle and you wouldn't have to backtrack much to follow his trail. However, without the actual riddle, you might not catch the shell's location and miss it while simply following their path.

In the quiet, Marius Jack pulls out a tiny container of oil from inside his doublet and hauls one of his fire-dried boots over onto his lap. He proceeds to work oil into the leather with a soft cloth while humming a low, contented song.

To find Marius Jack's portal, go to page 43
To follow Nessen and Mia, go to page 53

Marius Jack limps with each step, leaning on your shoulder for support.

When you woke that morning, he was sitting against a rock staring at his feet. He'd slowly, painfully drawn one knee up to his chest before letting it back down and repeating the process with the other knee.

"They're moving," you said, hoping to encourage him.

He'd given you a wobbly smile. "But I won't be able to walk without help. Not for a while yet, anyway." And the look on his face told you that deep inside, he was terrified of being left behind.

"We'll search for your pops' portal," you told him and a slow, relieved grin had brightened his expression.

Now, hours later, he's improved to the point where he can mostly carry his own weight, but he's still wobbly and you continue to offer your shoulder for support.

As you walk, Marius Jack regales you with stories about his pops, oblivious to the brush of wind against your faces. At every small gust, however, your own nerves tingle like someone's trailing a feather over your skin and unease sits like a stone in your belly.

"My nana always told the story of Isbell Island in a whisper, like it was some great secret.

She'd say—" he pauses as you aid him through a particularly swampy section of grass and sand. "She'd say pops got the assignment by lottery because no one wanted to get stuck out here. Previous stewards disappeared, never to be heard from, or seen, again."

You've heard of those stories but never put much thought into them. Now, you have your suspicions that they're true. You whip your head around at a hissing sound, but then you spot a disgruntled iguana and relax.

"My pops came back alive," Marius Jack continues, unaware of your unease or the iguana, "but he almost never spoke of the place other than to say it's a haven for monsters." Suddenly, he points ahead. "There! The portal's in the horse's head outcropping above the falls."

You've been following the northern side of the river all morning. Now, up ahead, the water disappears over a cliff with a mighty roar. Two jumbles of rocks stand as sentinels on either side where the earth drops away. The one closest to you indeed looks similar to the silhouette of a horse's head turned to the side.

"Where in the rocks?" you ask.

"Through the nostril."

The spot that looks like the nostril is a cave about the size of a rounded shield. You give Marius Jack a quizzical glance, wondering if he'll fit inside.

He shrugs his shoulders all the way to his ears. "Pops was running from a gator and saw the hole, so he crawled inside and, poof, ended up somewhere else."

Then, with dawning realization, Marius Jack glances at himself and his excitement vanishes. "I'm going to further destroy my clothes, aren't I?"

"Pants and boots at least," you say and he groans.

You leave him to his misery while you inspect the tiny cave for signs of animal habitation. There are none. Resigned, you crawl inside the dank musty space.

With a sigh, Marius Jack follows.

Moss squishes beneath you and acts like a water-logged sponge, soaking the knees and shins of your pants.

"I loved this outfit," Marius Jack whimpers.

"Need you to stay quiet now," you say.

"Right," he whispers.

You continue forward and hear him muffling his groans of distaste.

A flash of light startles you and the moss vanishes to be replaced by the grit of dry sand under your knees and palms.

Portal, you remind yourself as you continue forward and a new, cool wind smelling of ocean brine and magnolia flowers presses against you. The feathery touch turns your nerves to sensitive fire and you shudder, unsure if it's caused by the portal's magic or something else.

Suddenly, the tunnel ends, meeting with the edge of a dark lake with a vast cavern beyond. The tingling sensation runs over your arms, causing gooseflesh.

Marius Jack bumps into you.

"Sorry," he says softly.

Light dances in from an entrance across the glittering lake, highlighting the water but casting the walls into barely visible shadows. You narrow your eyes, spotting a couple darker sections in those walls that might be other portal entrances. Then your scan stops on a familiar shape on the far side of the lake.

Patricia's dark hair hangs around her face and her bejeweled fingers trail in the water. She's utterly still, and you wonder if she's dead, but then her fingers twitch, stirring small ripples in the water.

Seeing no other option to get to her, you crawl out of the tunnel and into the lake, instantly sinking to your hips. The subtle tingling you've felt since arriving on the island turns to sharp ice, freezing your legs.

Step, you try to convince them to move, but your muscles don't respond.

Behind you, Marius Jack tumbles out of the tunnel and gasps.

"For the love of velvet capes!" he wheezes.

You wonder if Patricia trapped you but she remains unnaturally still on the lakeshore, and horror fills her expression when you begin to shrink. Soon the water covers your stomach and, a moment later, the icy touch is at your chin.

Before you can process this further, you're standing on the bottom of the lake, no bigger than the menagerie of shells mottling the ground. Out of reflex, you're holding your breath, but behind you, Marius Jack exclaims,

"Sashes and scarves, I forgot! Pops said not to touch the water!"

You look back to find he's nudging a conch with his toe. It doesn't budge as he's smaller now than the heavy shell.

"Now you remember?" you ask, chancing a breath after seeing him speak. The air tastes sharp like after lightning strikes nearby, but otherwise you're able to breathe normally.

He winces but his dismay is quickly replaced by open-mouthed wonder as he points. "Look."

A shimmer of gold sits nestled amidst the red and black and white of the other shells. You move toward it. Everything grates beneath your feet, reminding you of hiking a mountainside full of shifting shale, but finally you find yourself staring down at the rich golden top of a clamshell.

You run your fingertips over its smooth, cool surface. For a moment, you hope it'll make you human-sized again, but nothing happens. Perhaps the shell doesn't recognize your being small as an illness to heal.

If you were human-sized, the shell wouldn't be bigger than your thumb nail. As it is, you'd barely be able to span it with your arms if you laid on top of it.

You glance at Marius Jack and an idea strikes you.

"We'll need your doublet," you say while you shrug out of your coat. "We're going to fashion a sling to carry the shell."

"Carry it?" He looks up, confused.

"Did you see Patricia?" You point to where you can barely see the tips of her fingers trailing in the water. "She's going to need it."

His lips form an "O" and he shucks out of his doublet.

"Drink it," Patricia insists.

You and Marius Jack stare dubiously at her where she sits weakly against the cavern wall. Within her hand she holds the remaining dust of the shell that healed her and now she's insisting that drinking the lake water will return you to your normal size.

All you can think about, however, is how freezing that water had been…and ending up the size of an ant.

"It's freezing," Marius Jack protests, echoing your thoughts.

"It'll make you big again," Patricia says. "Stop complaining."

"You're sure?" you ask, disturbed by your mousy voice.

She hesitates. "Reasonably sure," she finally admits with a shrug. "The myths indicate drinking the water's the key."

Marius Jack still hesitates, fingering the buttons on his shirt while staring at the dark lake.

The worst it can do, beyond freezing you into an icicle, is shrink you even more. You brace yourself and dip your hands into the water. Instantly the cold freezes your fingers, locking them into their cupped position. You barely lift them out of the water, struggling to move anymore.

Marius Jack reaches out and pushes your frozen palms to your lips and you take a small sip. Then, seizing on the opportunity, he tilts your hands so he can sip from them as well.

The water washes into your belly with a chill flush where it sits like a stone. Suddenly, there's a flash, and Patricia gives a whoop of excitement. Slowly, the chill recedes and you sit back, relieved to find yourself and Marius Jack normal again.

"Now, Hunter," Patricia says, "explain what this is all about. Perhaps I can help you."

You share a glance with Marius Jack and he shrugs. With a steadying breath, you dive into telling the storyteller the particulars, hoping she can help identify her poisoner, or, perhaps, find another shell.

The End

Jennifer M Zeiger

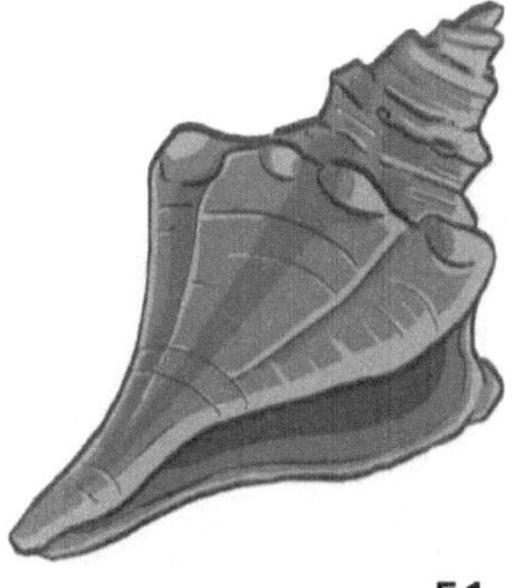

"I'll admit, I *was* disappointed when you decided to follow the scribe's trail instead of finding my pops' portal," Marius Jack says from where he sits on a palm log with his weak legs sprawled out in front of him. "But logic has prevailed and I'm now thinking you made the right choice."

You frown while you chew on a fig. When you woke that morning, he was sitting against a rock staring at his feet. He'd slowly, painfully drawn one knee up to his chest before letting it back down and repeating the process with the other knee.

"They're moving," you said, hoping to encourage him.

He'd given you a wobbly smile. "But I won't be able to walk without help. Not for a while yet, anyway." And the look on his face told you that deep inside, he was terrified of being left behind.

"I want to follow the scribe's trail," you told him. "I saw him headed west yesterday along the south bank. It'll require crossing the river, but you can join me if you want."

He'd stared at you, at first unbelieving that you would let him come along, but then a slow, relieved grin had brightened his expression.

Now, hours later, he's improved to the

point where he can mostly carry his own weight, but he's still wobbly and you continue to offer your shoulder for support.

"I'm serious as sashes," Marius Jack says. "My pops had to crawl to fit in the portal and I don't think I could manage that right now."

Chewing on another fig, you wonder if you should tell him the trail is about to get more challenging. If you listen closely, you can hear the distant roar of a waterfall and Mia's and Nessen's trail has been steadily heading in its direction all morning.

As you consider this, you realize you're staring at a print in the sand. It doesn't match the pockmarks of heels you've been following.

"Wait here," you say.

Marius Jack frowns, but then shrugs, and pulls a small, soft bristled brush from his pocket. He settles back and begins to work on the wrinkled velvet of his doublet while humming the song from the night before.

A brush? Here? You shake your head and follow the paw prints, leaving him to his task.

You crouch and lay a hand beside one fully formed print. *If it's a leopard, it's full grown,* you surmise. As far as you know, there aren't any other large felines in the region.

Not long after that, you find the remains of a small campsite and unease grows in your belly. Broken palm fronds litter the ground below a large tree that someone tried to climb. But deep gouges in the trunk attest to the feline's ability to climb and high above there's a swatch of fabric caught on the sharp end of a broken branch. It flutters in the breeze, revealing multi-colored patches sewn together.

Allen, the performer, you realize. *Guess he's no longer in the competition.*

To be sure, you search until you find a large swath of disturbed sand where the leopard dragged him away…in the direction of Mia and Nessen.

You hurry back to Marius Jack.

"What's wrong?" he asks as soon as he sees your face.

"Leopard," you say. "It got the performer and might be following Mia and Nessen."

The color drains from Marius Jack's face. He tucks his brush away and holds his hands out for you to help him rise, wobbling as he stands.

He doesn't protest the faster pace until you reach the cliffs where the river rushes into a cascading waterfall. Mia and Nessen clearly followed the steep incline down, and when Marius Jack peeks over the edge, he whimpers and takes a step behind you.

Letting him gather his nerve, you take in the falls to your right and the sparkling lake far below. The water shimmers with an iridescent bluish-purple hue and your nerve endings tingle in that now familiar way.

Magic. But you're not sure if it's the wind gusting over the cliffs or the odd shimmer of the water that's causing your reaction.

"That's um—" Marius Jack tries to glance over the edge of the cliffs again and swallows hard. "Like red shirts clashing with pink jackets, it makes my stomach queasy."

"Then face the cliff and don't look down while we descend."

"Face the cliff. Right. I can do that."

Starting down the steep incline, you pause long enough to see Marius Jack lean into the rock wall as he follows. It's a narrow pathway and even you find yourself stepping sideways to avoid crossing your feet.

"Don't look, don't look, don't…" Marius Jack mutters in a constant refrain.

You're about thirty feet from the bottom when a sound drifts upward on the wind. You pause and Marius Jack's chanting goes silent.

"Singing?" he asks.

"Mia and Nessen," you place the sweet tones of Mia's soprano and below it, Nessen's surprisingly even tenor. "They're under the waterfall," you say, figuring out why the song wavers and yet carries, muffled one moment and clear the next.

Nessen's riddle must have something to do with this, you think, and continue down to the bottom of the cliff.

Finally reaching the lake's edge, you scan the ground for any hint of the leopard. The cliff pathway had been solid rock and you'd lost the feline's tracks when you descended.

Marius Jack groans, lowering himself onto a rock to sit, but his moan dies mid-voice.

"What's that?" He points.

You follow his gesture and spot the dark, sleek form of a leopard crouched on the rocks across the lake. It's fixated on the falls, waiting for Mia and Nessen to emerge.

You realize their singing has stopped.

"Shout for them as soon as you see them," you tell Marius Jack, knowing he's too weak still to race around the lake with you.

You take off for the far side of the lake, weaving through cypress and palm trees along the way. Mia and Nessen already survived one attack from the leopard, but still you keep glancing across the lake, hoping the scribe and cook will appear on Marius Jack's side.

Finally, you spot them as they emerge from behind the falls, walking on a ledge of rock above the water's surface. Their heads are bent near each other and, even as far away as you are, you can see their elation at whatever Mia's holding.

A shell. At least, that's what you assume, but you're more concerned with their direction of travel. They keep walking, oblivious to the leopard now tensed to pounce as they draw near.

You're too far away yet to help them.

"Hey! Hey! Watch out! Hey!" Marius Jack's voice breaks as he shouts.

Nessen's head shoots up and he sees the dresser pointing.

He turns in time to spot the leopard launching itself off the rocks above. And the thin, ferret-like man shoves Mia away before the massive mottled leopard crashes into him. There's a sharp *crack* but you're not sure what caused it.

Mia screams, scrambling away, and you race past her while reaching for the knife in your boot. Against a leopard, it's a poor weapon, but the feline's distracted and you tackle it from the side. Your weight shoves it off of Nessen and gives you the leverage you need to drive your knife into its neck.

Your momentum carries you into the lake. Water washes over your head as a tingle runs from the roots of your hair to the tips of your toes. Pushing to the surface, you prepare to keep fighting but when your head breaks into the air and you gasp, the expected attack doesn't come. Finally, you spot the leopard floating limply away.

"Nessen!" Mia cries.

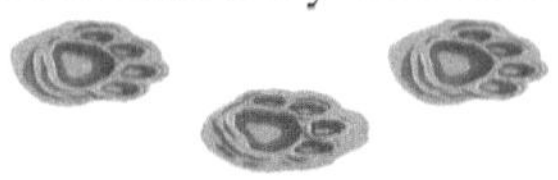

"Leave off," Nessen grumbles, pushing Mia's hands away to show her the cracked pen case in his breast pocket that took the brunt of the leopard's attack. "I'll be fine as a quill soon enough. Go help our rescuer."

Mia scans the water, but her eyes pass right over where you're floating.

"Uncle Nessen," she says, "where—?"

You begin swimming hard for the shore, positive now that the lake must indeed contain some sort of magic. Finally, Mia spots you when you reach the sand and climb from the water.

"Oh dear." She crouches and holds out her palm, which you immediately climb onto. You're no bigger than her longest finger. "You've been shrunk by the sauce."

You stand on the counter in the galley of the *King's Justice* having a staring contest with Robert, the King's Hand, overtop Mia's glittering golden shell.

He's the first one to look away.

Mia, Nessen, and Marius Jack sleep in hammocks farther back in the ship. Even still, Robert keeps his voice low.

"The island's dangerous," he says, "and you want me to send you back?"

"You promised the island to whoever found a shell first. I know you; you're going to follow through. I can't exactly protect the Alder forest like this," you motion at your three-inch-tall self, "but I can help Mia stay safe on Isbell Island."

Robert sighs. "Suppose you're right. And maybe you can find a cure to your—" he waves at you, "current condition. I'll go write out the orders."

The End

A snap decision has you racing toward the scribe and the cook. They work within the palace and are unlikely to have any experience facing a large predator.

The familiar leather-wrapped handle of your knife is in your grasp before you even think about pulling it, experience guiding you while you tear past pine and palm trees, pushing aside dangling moss and snaking vines along the way. It's a poor weapon against a leopard, but it's more than Mia and Nessen have.

As you break into the small clearing, you see Mia cowering against a large cypress, clutching a dead branch before her. Nessen stands between her and the leopard, holding a slender pen case as a weapon, and the leopard prowls from side to side with its sleek mottled fur glistening in the sunlight.

It flicks its ears, but it doesn't even glance over before bunching its hind quarters and lunging for the scribe.

He swings, shattering the pen case across the big cat's nose with a sharp *crack*, before disappearing in a mass of limbs and fur.

Still running, you hit the seventy-pound leopard in the side, shoving it off of the scribe before it can chomp down. Beneath your hands, a guttural, angry roar vibrates through the feline's chest and then it spins, swiping at you with a huge paw. Claws rip through your pants and tear into your thigh.

For a moment, you meet Mia's bright green gaze over the leopard's back. Her eyes are filled with terror, but also anger, and instead of staying back, she steps forward, raising her dead branch.

Then the pain registers and your knees collapse. You hit the sand but raise your knife even as the pain threatens to paralyze you.

There's a *thud* and the leopard huffs, spinning on Mia, who smacked it with her long branch.

As the feline spins, you pull back your arm and throw. A second later, you hear the low *thump* of your knife hitting home. The cat's body goes limp but its momentum carries it forward to crash into Mia and she falls beneath its massive form. After a moment of shocked silence, she shoves the feline away and emerges with her owl-white hair in disarray around her face.

"Hold still," Nessen scolds, his motions stiff due to the bandages on his left arm where the leopard's claws gouged his skin.

You jerk, swallowing a cry, when he

tightens a length of cloth torn from Mia's long skirts around your thigh. *Breathe*, you remind yourself as you notice Mia returning from the river.

"Anything?" you ask her.

"I'm sorry," she says. "I didn't find Marius Jack. The river must have carried him away."

You're tempted to ask her to search again, but she's so crestfallen that you can't bring yourself to speak the words.

"We'll stay the night here," Nessen says, finishing your bandage and moving to sit beside Mia against the gnarled roots of a towering oak. You suspect the leopard was the area's prime predator, so you relax against a slender pine.

Mia produces a loaf of brown bread from her small pack and tears off chunks to share.

"Following us?" Nessen asks, his nose twitching while he eyes you.

This seems obvious, so you don't answer. Instead, you pull out the oranges and figs you gathered from the ship and offer them.

A thrilled smile breaks across Mia's face and she accepts, forcing an orange into Nessen's long fingers when he doesn't immediately take one.

"It turned out to be a good thing, Uncle,"

she says. "We'd be burnt toast otherwise."

He snorts and turns his attention to peeling the orange with a pen knife he salvaged from his shattered pen case.

You pull another fruit from your pocket and realize it's the mandarin the performer threw at you. It's squishy from being overripe, but should still be edible. With a shrug, you dig a nail into the rind and it squirts sweet, citrusy juice into the air.

Mia's head comes up, her nostrils flaring as she sniffs. "Is that your mandarin?"

You're not sure what she's asking, so you hold it out to her.

She takes the fruit and holds it to her nose, breathing deeply. "This one's gone bad," she says, handing it back.

You finish peeling the rind off until you can pull apart the internal sections to investigate. At first, all you smell is the overly sweet citrus odor that first alerted Mia. But as you peer closer, you notice tiny black dots near the center of the fruit.

Poison? Using a test you practice in the forest to make sure you don't eat a bad mushroom or other plant, you break open one of the slices to expose the juice inside and touch it to your tongue.

Usually, the test requires waiting for several hours, but within minutes, the tip of your tongue begins to go numb.

You spit and set the mandarin aside, positive now that it's not just overripe.

You recall the performer, Allen, tossing the mandarins at Patricia and yourself. And you also recall Marius Jack eating another one at the rail of the ship. It wasn't long after that, maybe half a day, before he keeled over into the river.

Tearing off a chunk of Mia's bread, you savor its rich nutty flavor while staring at the bad mandarin and considering what to do next. Around you the buzz of bugs and croak of frogs fills the air. In the distance, a high-pitched cackling breaks the calm of the campsite and the nearby wildlife goes silent.

You pause, tilting an ear as you try to place what kind of creature makes such a sound.

"What was that?" Mia whispers.

"Goblins maybe," you say around a bite of bread, "or sprites."

Mia shivers and Nessen wraps a long arm around her shoulders while scowling at you.

"Are you going with us in the morning?" Mia asks. "I'd feel safer if you did."

You pause with your last piece of bread

almost to your mouth.

Nessen glares, but Mia gazes at you in wide-eyed hope.

As the wind brushes your skin and brings with it that ever-present shiver of magic, you admit Mia and Nessen would be safer if you stayed with them. As far as you can tell, they can't even sense the magic wafting through the very breath of the island.

You shove the last bite into your mouth to give yourself a second before answering and your eyes snag on Nessen's leather-bound book, barely visible in his jacket pocket. With his riddle, there's hope they'll find a shell, but will they make it back to the ship with the dangers of the island surrounding them?

And, you admit, the island's not the only danger. There's the matter of Allen. You keep from glancing at the poisoned mandarin sitting on the ground beside you, but it irks you that he'd use a fruit of all things to poison someone. Now that you're sure Allen's the poisoner, it'd be prudent to track him down before he poisons someone else.

———————————————

To protect Mia and Nessen, go to page 71
To track down Allen, go to page 81

"She broke out in such hives, I swear she didn't even look like the Queen anymore, like how a burnt cake no longer looks like a cake but a lump of charcoal instead. And, of course, everyone knew I was the one who prepared…"

After a morning of traveling with Mia and Nessen, you now know Mia can talk for hours without seeming to breathe. It's a talent you've never seen before.

"Mia," Nessen cuts in when she stumbles on the steep path in the cliff face.

The scribe's riddle led to the top of a long cliff over which the river cascades with a mighty roar into a treed stretch of land below. The water lands, frothing in a lake that shimmers with a bluish-purple tinge. Every time your gaze lands on it, your nerves tingle like a feather's brushing your skin and you wonder if the wild magic of the island is extra concentrated in its glittering depths.

Mia steadies herself and keeps talking as she continues down. "…and Uncle Nessen didn't even hear about my mistake and the Queen's reprimand until that evening because he was serving his own punishment out in the public library for spilling ink on the Queen's favorite rug. She almost docked his pay to cover its cost, but apparently…"

You follow behind her on the narrow

pathway, stepping sideways to keep from crossing one foot over the other while you listen. The motion pulls at the bandage on your leg, making the wound beneath burn. As you near the bottom of the cliff, you draw closer to the waterfall and its roar begins to cut into Mia's words.

"…he's…to clean…but…not…"

Nessen leads the way, following whatever riddle his book contains about Isbell Island. Mia almost explained it over breakfast, but Nessen shot her a warning scowl and instead she launched into a detailed description about pastry making using butter and cherry jam.

"…I've heard…to use…lemon…"

You're not even sure what Mia's talking about now.

Nessen stops and his hand shoots out to grasp Mia's shoulder. She goes silent.

Without her talking, the thunder of the falls becomes everything and intermixed in its roar is a squeaky, high-pitched melody. It makes you think of a drunken goblin singing off-key.

Mia and Nessen share a look and before you can react, they're both tearing down the last thirty feet of trail to reach the bottom of the cliff.

Surprise keeps you still for an extra-long moment. The last time you rushed into an unknown area, you ran headlong into a giant bird's nest only to find the screeching you heard was the chicks begging for food.

You almost shout after them, shocked their encounter the day before doesn't make them more cautious, but they're too far away now to hear over the thunder of the water.

As you reach the bottom of the cliffs, you resist the urge to hurry after them and instead pause to scan the area. The lake shimmers, continuing to make your nerves shiver. The wind smells of damp earth and tree bark and the singing that's still coming from behind the falls no longer sounds like a goblin. You try to think of something it reminds you of, but all that comes to mind is a mouse belting out a happy melody.

Mia and Nessen disappear behind the waterfall by way of a small ledge of damp rock. You dearly hope whatever or whoever is singing doesn't mind company.

Your eyes travel away from the cascading falls, over the iridescent lake, and past the trees, and then sweep along the cliff again. Something glints with the familiar reflectiveness of metal high up on the trail and you see the flutter of clothing caught in the wind as someone moves along the path.

The movement is furtive in the same way a snow cat stalks its prey.

Since you're still standing near the forest that grows thick along the base of the cliffs, it's a matter of a few steps to tuck yourself into the shadows of the foliage.

You pull your boot knife free and test its weight on your palm while the ever present wind flutters the leaves around you. It carries the roar of the falls but no longer contains the squeaky singing.

Above, the stealthy figure continues to move closer. Whoever it is has flipped their hood over their head and is holding their jacket tight to their body.

Out of the corner of your eye, you catch Mia and Nessen emerging from behind the falls. As far as you can tell, no one else comes with them.

The person coming down the trail crouches, aiming a crossbow at the unknowing pair. The motion flares the person's coat, revealing multi-colored patches on pants.

Allen.

The crossbow bolt's heavy metal tip glints in the sunlight as Allen shifts to track his targets.

"Hey!" you shout with the same deep holler you use to bellow back at bears or trolls.

Both Mia and Nessen look over. Nessen

swings an arm around Mia's thin shoulders even as she protests and clutches something protectively in her hand.

The performer, for his part, doesn't respond as he sights down the bow.

You race forward despite the burn in your wounded leg and wish Allen had reached the bottom of the cliff before Mia and Nessen emerged. As it is, he still stands some fifteen feet up the trail, giving him the height advantage.

Just like attacking a troll, you think as you throw your knife. The weapon was never made to be thrown, and it tumbles end over end in a wobbly arc.

A second later, Allen lurches, crying out, and the crossbow *snaps,* releasing its bolt.

Allen tumbles down the trail in a cloud of dust and flying limbs. At the same time, the bolt disappears into the waterfall over Nessen's head, jerked off target a second before Allen pulled the trigger.

Before fully tumbling off the trail and plummeting the last eight feet to the ground, Allen catches himself and jumps, flipping through the air before landing on his feet.

Your stomach sinks but then Allen cries out and crumbles as his ankle gives way. He rolls back and forth, clutching his leg and shouting in anger.

You pull a cord from one of your many pockets as you approach to tie him up.

"Oh! You saved our toast again!" Mia rushes over, holding out her hands like a child to show you whatever treasure she's found.

You expect a shell.

Instead, you see a small figure sitting on her palms. It's a moment before you recognize Marius Jack with his green doublet and dark hair.

"I've got a few grievances against this contest!" Nessen announces, coming up beside Mia. "First of all, did you know the lake here shrinks people? And second, contestants should not be allowed to poison or threaten each other! How did this man get a crossbow?"

"Stole it off the ship," you say, remembering the empty slot in the weapons rack.

"Marius Jack is paralyzed from the waist down! What do you have to say for yourself?" Nessen demands of your prisoner.

Before Allen can respond, however, Marius Jack speaks up in a high squeak. "Look, I found a shell!" And he holds out his palm to show everyone his treasure.

Nessen pinches his nose. "And that's my last grievance."

The deck of the *King's Justice* sways beneath your feet as Robert, the King's Hand, comes to stand beside you at the rail.

"You're headed back to search for Patricia?" he asks.

You think of Marius Jack's reaction to the poison. You're fairly sure Patricia was poisoned too and it doesn't sit well that she's somewhere on the island, probably paralyzed.

You nod and a short silence falls while you watch the water slap against the ship's hull below.

"Nessen's furious," Robert finally says, chuckling, "that after washing over the cliffs, shrinking in the lake, and somehow surviving to crawl out below the falls, Marius Jack accidentally found a shell by singing his joy at being alive. He says the shell simply fell out of the falls onto his head."

You grunt and accept the mango Robert passes to you.

"You know the irony of it all?"

You raise a brow.

"The very shell Marius Jack found could heal his paralysis, except someone didn't gift it to him, so it won't work."

You think about this. "Will it work again?" you ask around a slice of fruit. "Can another shell be found by singing below the falls?"

A slow grin pulls at Robert's lips. "It just might."

You cut off another slice of mango, but before you bite into it you say, "Guess I'm not just going back to find the storyteller then."

The End

Jennifer M Zeiger

Mia's shoulders drooped when you told her you won't be staying with her and Nessen. But the smell of the mandarin and the memory of Marius Jack keeling over into the river keeps playing through your mind. So you say goodbye and head back toward the cove where the *King's Justice* dropped you off.

The bandages on your wounded leg pull and the wound burns, but it's not so bad as to prevent you from walking. Above, the island's birds chatter, unconcerned about you passing below like a jungle cat winding through the trees. You realize Robert's genius in gathering the suspects of the Queen's poisoning and setting before them a prize worth killing for.

It encouraged Allen to poison again.

The ever present breeze ruffles your hair and carries to you a new scent. Something that doesn't belong even amidst the magic laden air. You stop, breathing deeply just like Mia did with the mandarin the night before. There's sweet magnolias, briny ocean, damp earth…and cold smoke.

Following that last scent, you step into a small campsite. It harbors the remains of a smoldering fire. Someone snuffed it out with the sandy dirt but small whisps of smoke still drift above the black coals.

Already knowing where Mia and Nessen were last night, you also rule out Marius Jack. If he's alive, he's much farther downstream. That leaves Patricia and Allen, except you're fairly certain Patricia ate a poisoned mandarin as well, which would make her incapable of building, and then snuffing, a campfire. So, unless there's someone on the island you don't know about, the fire belonged to Allen.

You shudder. The deadly performer camped not far from where you slept the night before and the only reason you didn't catch the scent of smoke was because of the direction of the wind. You hadn't camped close enough to the river for it to carry sound or smell to you.

Did he hear us talking?

Immediately, your mind goes to Mia. The cook had talked the evening away, bubbly as a chattering squirrel. The chances Allen didn't hear her are small.

The sandy loam and trees around the campsite still hold the tale of Allen's evening. Scuff marks below the magnolias show where he gathered the wood for the fire. A matted pile of dead leaves tells you where he slept. And then deep gouges in the dirt attest to him digging up handfuls to quench the coals in the morning. Finally, you spot the rounded pockmarks from his boots, showing which way he headed after his breakfast.

Those prints lead you back the way you

came until they veer toward the river where he stopped and knelt to drink. On the riverbank, his knees pressed rounded dots in the sand.

That's why I didn't run into him this morning, you realize.

You continue tracking his heel marks, which unerringly head toward Mia and Nessen until his prints overlap those of the scribe and cook.

You hope, after their encounter with the leopard, that they might be more cautious in their travels, but a sense of doubt has you hurrying to catch up.

It's not long before you make out voices downstream. With the river carrying sound away from you, the voices have to be raised for you to hear them and you wince when you recognize Mia's soprano raised in a shout. Even still, you can't make out her words yet.

Hurrying closer, dread builds in your stomach as you make out two other sounds.

One is the dull roar of a waterfall, and the other the scratchy, loud voice of Allen, the performer.

"Don't move."

"We'll give you whatever you want," Mia squeaks.

"Mia," Nessen scolds. "There's no reason

he won't kill you after we give him what he wants."

You slow, thinking. From their voices, you know they're right on the riverbank. To keep Allen from spotting you, you angle into the trees and approach in a slow stalk.

"You're not dumb," Allen chuckles. "But here's the rub. I'll for sure kill her if you *don't* give me what I want."

You stop moving when you spot Mia's owl-white hair through the trees. Allen grips her around the waist, holding a knife to her throat with his other hand. Behind them, the river froths and gurgles in its headlong rush into a waterfall not far beyond.

From the sound of his voice, Nessen's to your left in the trees, but you can't see him.

"That puts us in the ink, doesn't it?" Nessen says. "Because if you kill her, I'll never tell you where to find a shell."

Allen bares his teeth, realizing he's at an impasse with the scribe.

You finger your golden justice medallion, its surface smooth in your grasp. It doesn't look perfectly like a shell, but the shape's close.

Pulling the medallion off over your head, you remove its strap. Then you call as you step out of the trees, "I'll make a deal with you."

The performer's head whips around and his body

shifts to angle Mia between you two.

"I'll make a deal," you say again, holding your hand up with the back to him. Then you splay your fingers wide so the gold of the medallion shows through without revealing its shape.

"Oh! You found—"

Mia cuts off with a whimper as Allen presses his knife tighter to her neck.

He fixates on the gold showing through your fingers and you give him just enough time to see the shimmer before you tuck the medallion away into your jacket.

"Give me the—"

Allen doesn't finish as Nessen hits him from the side. All three of them stumble, flailing in a mass of limbs. Their path heads straight for the steep bank of the frothing, rushing river beyond. There's first one splash as Allen tumbles in and then a second as Mia follows immediately after.

"No!" You race forward, catching Nessen's arm before he follows them and hauling him back onto land.

"Mia! Mia's in there!" the scribe yells, trying to dive into the roaring river.

You shove him back onto the sand while scanning the water for Mia's distinctive hair. Finally, you spot her head breaking the surface. She gasps but the weight of her skirt pulls her back down and when she resurfaces, she's closer to the falls despite her arms churning against the river's current.

"Follow me," you order, shucking out of your coat as you go.

Nessen follows. Nearer the falls, you spot Mia again and pull your knife from your boot. You hold it just right so as not to slice yourself open when you jump.

"Be ready to snag her," you say before diving into the river.

Your aim's true. When you surface, your hands tangle in Mia's skirt. You begin cutting it away and have her freed of the sodden fabric when you notice Allen disappear over the fast approaching mist of the falls.

Spluttering, you push Mia toward Nessen's side of the river. For a second, this shoves your head underwater and you lose hold of her.

Coming back up, you spot Nessen laying on his stomach on the rocks, his arms reaching frantically for his niece while the river carries her along.

He's not close enough. You kick to reach Mia again and give her one last shove toward her uncle, seeing their hands catch a moment before you sail out over the cliffs.

Robert leans against the rail of the *King's Justice*, staring at the smooth golden shell and the

King's justice medallion resting in his palm. With a thumb, he catches the tears escaping his eyes.

Nessen comes to stand beside him, placing his slender, ink-stained fingers on the teak.

"Mia and I wouldn't be alive without your hunter," he says.

They searched at the base of the falls, but only found Marius Jack, who somehow survived his own tumble over the cliffs but had been shrunken by the lake below. Still, he'd figured out Nessen's riddle by accident and had been holding the golden shell when they found him.

"One of the best hunters I've ever known," Robert replies.

"I'm thinking a hero's burial might be in order?" Nessen suggests.

Robert hums his agreement. "My thoughts exactly."

The End

Allen's probably right. The hut's so obvious from the beach that it's likely been picked clean by anyone searching for the golden shells.

You rush to catch up with the performer, who's striding away toward the western side of the island with a spring in his step and a whistle on his lips. When he enters the tall grass of the sand dunes, his steel-colored hair disappears.

You lengthen your stride, stepping through the grass in the trail he left behind until, a moment later, you spot him again.

"…went this way too," he's saying as you catch up, "and now they've got a head start on us."

You fall into step beside him and he glances over. "The scribe and cook, they're no real problem," he continues. "Never out of doors, you see. The heat will burn the cook's poor complexion lobstery. It's the other two though—" he wags a finger and leaves his thought hanging.

You enter the shade of the pines and magnolias and a cool breeze presses against your skin. It brings gooseflesh along your arms but you ignore it as something catches your eye.

Now that you're out of the tall grass, the forest floor has turned into a soft, fragrant loam filled with moldering leaves and patches of sand.

It's perfect for leaving tracks and several sets of prints are pressed into the earth. You crouch to inspect them.

"Leaping pirouettes!" Allen exclaims, "Warn a fellow when you're stopping." He spins, clutching his long coat tight, and watches you inspect the trail. A frown grows between his bushy brows. "I still can't place you. Where'd you say you work again?"

At least you're expecting the question this time. Instead of answering, you point and say, "The scribe and cook came this way. And one other wasn't far behind them."

"A game warden?" Allen guesses, cocking his head. Then your words register. "*Three* of them came this way? Well, that won't do! When the show's crowded, no one owns the stage!"

He cups his chin, tapping his whiskered cheek with a finger. "We'll go the other way," he finally says. "To the cave picture instead."

"That's that way." You point to the northeastern part of the island, although you're wondering why he's including you.

He spins, letting his coat fly out in a circle, to head northeast. He pushes thick vines and clusters of jasmine out of his way as he goes, filling the air with their scent. Absently, you note the warblers are silent in the trees above.

It's not long before Allen's springy step turns into a shuffling trudge and sweat begins to soak all the way through his shirt and into his jacket between his shoulder blades. He still clutches the garment close despite the heat as the trail begins to lead upward.

The childlike sketch in the hut had indicated the cave sits high on the slopes of a rocky hill and you can now confirm its accuracy.

Allen's breath puffs in and out and he shoots you a jealous glare at your own even breathing.

"Blistering bottoms!" he exclaims, not for the first time. "I can *feel* the blisters growing with each step. You planned this! You wanted Allen weakened. Maybe you plan to take the shell when I find it?" He shoots you another suspicious glance but then has to look forward again to keep from stumbling.

You don't respond but you do catch his arm when he trips.

Jerking away, he stops and straightens up, arching his back to pop it while his sweat-stained jacket flutters around his legs.

Why's he still wearing it?

"No shell for you!" he shouts, pointing a finger in your face. "We find one, Allen gets it. You can't tire me enough to convince me otherwise." His words bounce off the rocks, ricocheting over the hillside.

You wonder what he'd do if you argued, but before you can think on it further, you hear the scraping of rock sliding against rock.

"You think you're so smart," he keeps shouting, waving his arms, but your attention's no longer on him.

There's more scraping, then a faint *whomp*.

Your stomach sinks as you wait, hoping not to hear another *whomp*.

A moment later, *whomp*, and you're sure.

"Move!" you shout, diving for Allen when glistening blue and red wings appear over the ridge ahead. They easily span a couple hundred feet, attesting to the size of the roc, or bird, they're attached to.

Allen jerks away again, suspicion drawing his heavy brows tight. He reaches into his coat and you see the curved wood of a crossbow beneath. Before he can raise it, you catch him and drive him to the ground. The crossbow flies from his grasp. A second later, the roc's talons dig into the dirt where he'd been standing.

As the bird wings away, Allen's crossbow peeks through its thick talons. Suddenly, those massive claws clench and the bow snaps into pieces.

Dropping the shattered weapon, the bird wheels around and dives, kicking up gusts of wind that shoves shards of loose rock over the ground. Allen squeaks and ducks, frozen in place by the sight.

Your stomach clenches. Without your bow or sword, you may as well be facing a scaled dragon. Frantically, you search for another option and spot a dark circle in the rocks ahead. It's perfect. The cave's too small to fit the roc, but big enough for two people.

"There," you point and haul Allen to his feet.

Whomp.

You shove him ahead while you dodge to the side. Thick talons snap the air beside your head and you go deaf for a moment as another *whomp* sounds above. The wind from the wings shoves you to your knees but you spot Allen scrambling up the path ahead, almost to the cave.

He'll make it, you think, and then he pauses, staring over the ridge where the roc originally appeared. A wicked grin pulls at his lips.

"Eggs!" he points, starting to move toward the nest instead of the cave.

Your stomach sinks when you realize his purpose. He intends to ward the bird off by holding one of her eggs hostage. But rocs are fiercely protective of their young and the bird's more apt to fly into a rage, killing you both and crushing her egg in the process without meaning to.

You race forward, trying to reach Allen before he gets too far, but you're not sure what you're going to do.

Shove him into the cave?

Protect the eggs from him?

Rocs aren't stupid. This one *might* back off if you show you're not going to hurt her young, but first you have to stop Allen.

You reach the crest of the ridge where the ground sinks into a deep bowl and find a mass of timbers, ripped sail cloth, and rusted metal that's been piled together into a massive nest.

Another gust of wind hits you and you stumble. Falling, you roll inward toward the collection of rubble. Only by splaying your arms wide do you stop yourself before tumbling headlong into the nest.

But a quick glance around shows you're now closer to the nest and its eggs than Allen. Above, Allen dodges and cartwheels beneath the roc's talons in his effort to get to an egg.

If you run at him, you might be able to shove him back toward the safety of the small cave beyond, but you're not sure you can reach him past the angry bird.

Now that you're closer to the nest, it might also be possible to intercept Allen from grabbing one of the giant blue and red mottled eggs. You're sure that would annoy the performer, but it might also calm the roc before she kills you both.

As you consider, the shimmer of a pond to your right catches your eye. Its dark waters beckon, offering safety in its shadowy depths. Maybe if Allen sees you hiding, he'll do the same?

To dive into the pool, go to page 97
To shove Allen toward the cave, go to page 101
To protect the roc's eggs, go to page 107

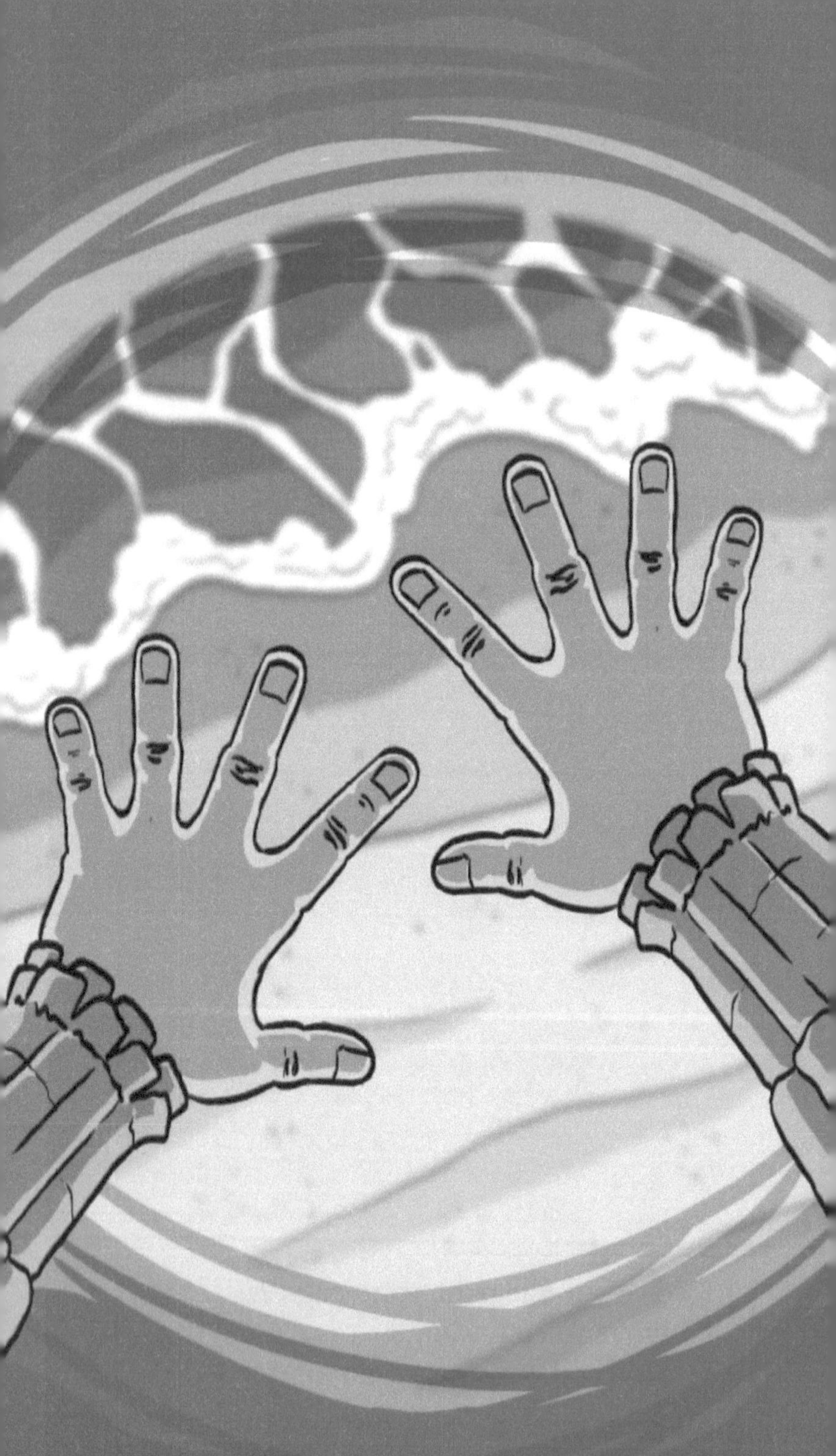

It'd be a huge gamble to reach Allen beneath the roc's talons and you're not sure about relying on the bird's good graces.

Hoping Allen sees you and realizes his plan to capture an egg is a terrible one, you pull in a deep breath and dive into the dark pool.

You expect the cold embrace of water, but instead, your nerves tingle with fire from the roots of your hair to the tips of your toes. A flush of heat washes over you and there's a sudden, brilliant flash of white light.

The world spins. At first, you're diving, but then bright daylight hits you and you realize the thing rushing at your face is gray and white sand.

At the last second, you tuck into a roll. Hitting the beach on your shoulder, you tumble, smacking into sharp debris scattered across the sand. Finally, you stop, sprawled amidst broken logs and planking, chunks of metal, and even huge feathers.

It looks like the remnants of an old shipwreck but from the iridescent blue and red feathers, you guess it's pieces from the roc's nest.

As things finally calm in your head, you wonder that you're not in a dark pool of water. You're not even wet.

Your eyes wander beyond the debris. Out beyond the surf, you spot the *King's Justice* at anchor in the bay. A longboat is rowing back toward it from the island.

Did Robert send them back for something?

You push to your feet and turn, just to make sure this is, in fact, the same beach where the *King's Justice* dropped you off. Not far away sits the bamboo hut. It's west instead of east, but still confirms you're in the same original area.

Then motion beyond the hut catches your eye. In the grass on the far side, the cook's owl-white hair and the scribe's hunched shoulders retreat beyond the low sand dunes and into the trees like they did earlier in the day.

You look down the beach where you stood before while watching everyone scatter, and stare as a hazy figure with a leather jacket and distinct pocketed pants simply fades away.

You sway, dizzy, while fighting a sense of unease. Once the vertigo passes, you tilt your head upward, feeling your nerve endings itch at what you're about to find.

Sure enough, you spot a faint shimmer in the air similar to a heat haze but it's shaped in a perfect circle.

A portal. You sway again. *And not just a*

transportation portal.

Seeing the cook and scribe walking away had been the first hint, seeing your hazy double fade had been the disturbing second, but now you see the sun hangs at the exact same location as where it sat when the longboat dropped you off that morning.

I went back in time. You shudder.

But then you pause. *Maybe this is a small gift,* you think. *I can pick my path again, except this time I have more information.*

You've already searched the hut, but you could go back to search the floor where you suspect there's a trapdoor. Otherwise, you can either follow the others or, you realize, you can head back toward the cave location now that you're aware of the giant bird.

To follow someone, go to page 27
To investigate the hut's floor, go to page 113
To head back to the cave, go to page 145

You race toward Allen. If you can shove him backward, he'll only be a few yards from the safety of the small cave.

Ahead and above you, he capers side to side and cartwheels below the roc to avoid its sharp talons. If you didn't spot the terror rounding his eyes, you'd think the performer was having fun. He yelps when the roc catches the back of his coat and lifts him off the ground.

He struggles, contorting until his arms slide free and he falls.

With a screech, the roc drops the garment and wheels around to come at him again. You reach Allen's side as you hear another *whomp* and a heavy gust of wind drives you to your knees.

"Twisted trapezes! I turned my ankle!" Allen cries.

Since he can't stand on his own, you haul his arm over your shoulder and lift him to his feet, smelling the wet stench of his sweat as you do. You're only a few feet from the safety of the cave, but he limps, leaning heavily on you as you move toward it.

He glances back and whimpers. "Faster!"

Gathering a last effort, you lunge and fall into the safety of the cave as the roc's long, three-pronged talons scrape against the rocks behind you.

"Not a big place," Allen waves at the cave walls. The setting sun hits the entrance, shining brilliant light to the back wall where you and Allen sit side by side.

"Big enough," you say while peeling a mandarin you had in your pocket. Your stomach growls at the smell of citrus filling the air. Running from a giant bird happens to be hungry business.

You savor the first bite, hunger making it taste sweeter than usual.

The roc tried twice more to reach inside the small cave before giving up. You haven't seen it since. Once nightfall hits, you plan to sneak away without the bird noticing.

You eat another slice and offer Allen a piece. He shakes his head, but holds up a finger and reaches into one of the many pockets on his colorful, patched pants.

"Those eggs," Allen says while he searches his pockets. "Those eggs would fetch a mighty fine price."

You snort. "At the cost of your life."

"True," he admits. Finally, he pulls out a metal flask from a red pocket. Then he produces, of all things, two small tankards.

"Found 'em in the hut," he says, grinning.

"And they didn't shatter?" You think of his fall from the roc's talons.

He cackles. "Must be made of magic!"

You shudder, but accept the tankard he offers. It feels like heavy glass, but you don't question it as he pours a little rum into your mug, and then pours some into his own.

"Let's celebrate," he says and lifts his tankard. "To surviving the day!"

You attempt to lift your mug but your muscles spasm and the tankard slips from your fingers. Rum splashes across the cave floor.

Confused, you stare at it, realizing your feet are numb and an odd flavor, like bitter cotton, coats your tongue.

Your eyes travel to the mandarin in your other hand and you realize, belatedly, that it's the same one Allen threw at you while on the *King's Justice*.

He's the poisoner, you realize too late.

He sees comprehension drain the color from your face. "Didn't see that finale coming, did you?" He chortles before knocking back his own drink in glee.

His chortle turns into a gurgle and his tankard hits the dirt.

Right before your eyes, the performer shrinks, becoming no bigger than a three-inch-tall bug.

"No! No! No!" he squeaks, hopping from one foot to the other, and then squealing as he hits the ground, clutching his rolled ankle.

You'd laugh, except now you can't feel your feet and your legs won't move. There's a faint tingling in your fingers but, thankfully, you can still move them. Maybe whatever poison you ingested isn't enough to fully paralyze you.

But in case it does, you don't want Allen running around free, even if he stays bug-sized.

With a monumental effort, you close your fingers around your empty tankard.

Allen's still rolling on the ground, ranting in wordless frustration.

Grunting, you flip the heavy tankard overtop him and rest your arm on top to keep him from lifting it.

With your lifeless legs, you can't sneak past the roc to return to the ship. Maybe the poison will wear off, but you doubt it. However, Robert only gave the contestants a couple of days to search for the shells. After that, you're sure he'll come find you, and you at least have the poisoner to give him.

Your stomach growls, still hungry. Taking advantage of the current use of your hands, you pull out the bag of figs you took from the ship and slowly eat them. You even take pity on Allen and slip one under the glass for him to eat.

Then, satisfied he can't get away, you settle in to wait.

The End

The pool of water glistens with a muted aqua glow. Even with the midday sun shining overhead, you can't see within its shimmering depths. You have no idea how deep it goes and so you discard the idea of diving into it. Then, gauging the distances between you, Allen, and the nest, you realize you're closer to the eggs than the performer and have a better chance of reaching them.

Higher on the hill, Allen ducks under the roc's reaching talons and cartwheels. Around him, dust whirls in the air from the giant bird's beating wings. You'd think he's having fun except his eyes are rounded in terror. Suddenly, he stumbles, but when his knees hit the ground, he keeps rolling, turning the mishap into a controlled tumble into the nest.

Panic spikes within you with how fast he's approaching the eggs. If he gets ahold of one, there'll be no saving the situation.

You slide, letting the loose sand carry you until you skid into the jumble of broken logs. Now that you're closer, you realize the long, straight poles are the remnants of broken ships' masts. But you don't have time to consider the implications of this as Allen finishes his roll and lunges for the cluster of three large eggs sitting in the middle of the heaped debris.

Crawling atop the upturned rectangle of a

large sea chest, you dive off it toward Allen. You slam into his side moments before his fingers brush the hard shell of the closest egg.

For a moment, you feel the heat coming off the massive eggs, but it vanishes when you fall into the jumbled mess of logs and metal beyond.

Allen shoves you, snarling, and climbs back toward the eggs again. You move to follow and pain radiates from your ankle. Your foot's snagged between a rock and a broken mast. You tug, but when it doesn't give, you contort around in time to snatch Allen's ankle, making him fall.

He spins, and you see the flash of a block, a ship's pulley, as he swings it at your head.

It doesn't land. There's another heavy *whomp* and the roc plucks Allen from amidst the nest's debris.

The giant bird wings higher with the performer struggling in its talons, which easily encircle his entire waist. Suddenly, the blue and red wings flare, stalling the roc midair, and it drops him— directly into the same pool of water you considered diving into earlier. There's no splash, no ripples from his fall, nothing.

Allen simply vanishes.

The roc lets out an echoing, triumphant screech. It turns and wings toward you, but you're still staring at the pool, waiting for Allen to surface.

Nothing.

Then wind from the roc's wings pelts your skin with sand and sharp splinters. You cower, expecting to feel the bird's talons next. Instead, there's a *thump* and you peek to find a huge golden eye considering you. The head turns side to side before the beak darts forward.

You cringe, but the roc merely pinches the broken mast in its powerful beak and pulls it away, freeing your foot.

Shocked, you crawl backwards until you can sit on top of a rock to take stock. Your ankle throbs and a trickle of blood leaks down your cheek from the debris scattered by the roc's wings. Otherwise, you seem to be in one piece. While you dab a cloth against your skin, the roc drops the broken mast with a ground-shaking thud. It then begins rooting around in the nest.

Now might be the best time to leave, you figure, so you climb to your feet to hobble away.

A piercing screech sets your nerves on edge and you glance back. The giant bird glares at you.

You prudently sit down again. Those huge golden eyes glare for a moment longer before the bird goes back to rooting under the far side of the nest. It comes out with a chunk of wooden planking, then a badly dented and rusted chest plate. A piece of a dresser follows and you begin to wonder what shipwreck the roc raided.

Finally, the bird rears up, clutching something in its beak. It turns to you but pauses over its multicolored eggs, swaying back and forth while eyeing you.

The message is clear. For protecting her eggs, she's giving you something.

When she leans forward, you hold out an open palm, hoping she doesn't take your hand off as you do.

The roc drops whatever's in her beak and backs away to hover over her eggs again.

A bright golden shell glitters on your palm. Reverently, you close your fingers around its cool texture.

Climbing to your feet again, you watch the roc to make sure it's okay with you leaving now. It doesn't object.

As you pass by, you pause long enough to peer into the dark pool where Allen disappeared. Now that you're not worried about the bird attacking or Allen stealing her eggs, you notice a shimmer like a bluish-purple haze over the water. Your nerve endings tingle with Isbell Island's unique signature of magic. Just to confirm, you find a rock and throw it in. There's no splash. No ripples. But after a second, you see a flash of light and then nothing again.

A portal? You guess.

The roc's head swings around and she gives a warning cry.

You hold up your hands, having pocketed the shell, and back away, limping toward the southern shore of the island where the *King's Justice* awaits your return.

The End

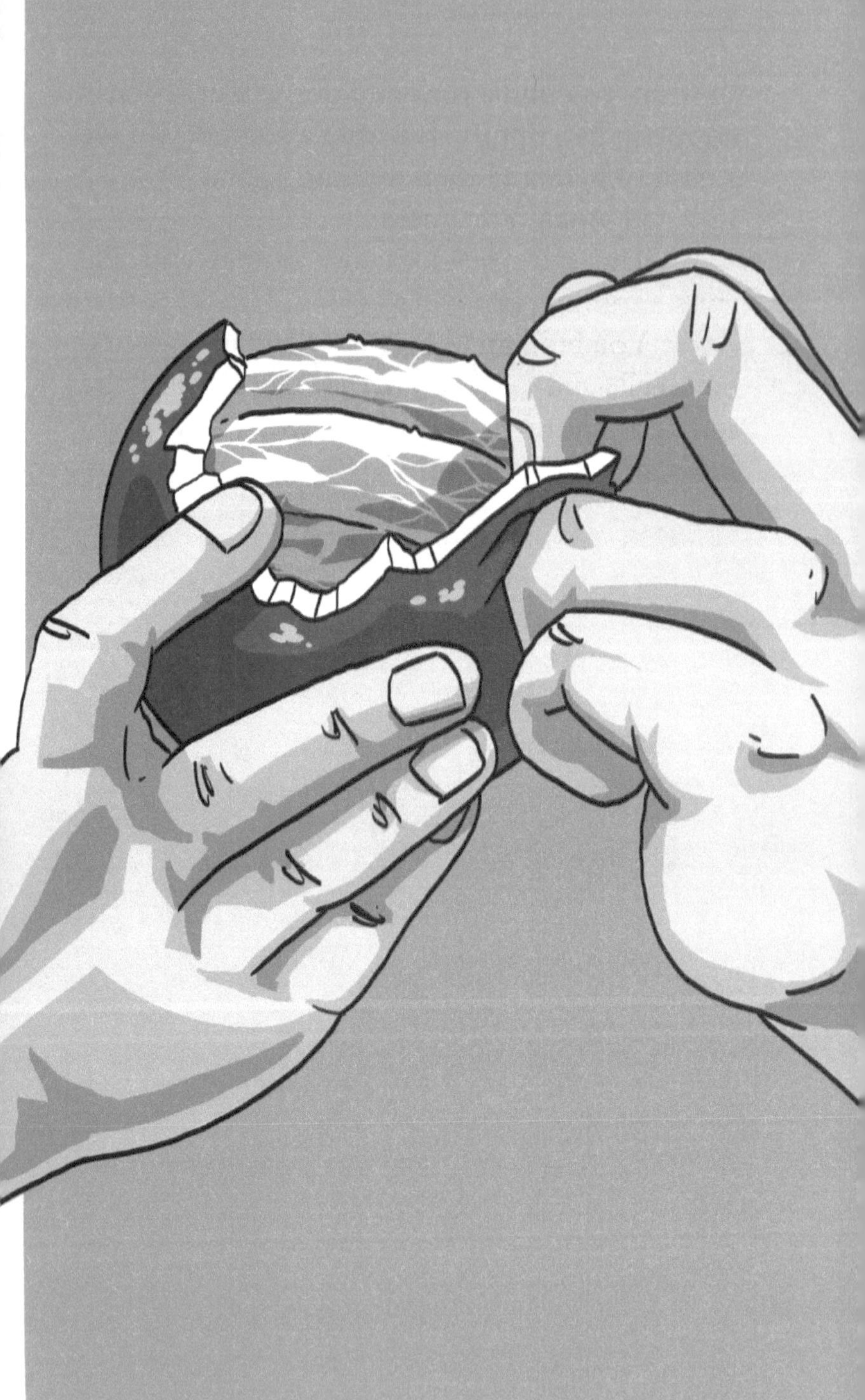

If events happen like they did earlier in the day, Allen will visit the hut to search it and then leave. Instead of immediately rushing in to investigate the floor then, you move off the beach into the tall grass on the dunes to wait outside.

Warblers chirp their high song in the trees before suddenly going silent, giving you a moment's warning before the steel-haired performer appears, clutching his long coat tight to his thin frame. Knowing what he conceals beneath it now, you make out the imprint of the crossbow he's carrying. He looks around and checks the footprints in the sand before heading to the hut.

As you listen to him rummage around, you pull out one of the oranges you found in the ship's galley and enjoy the snack until he reappears. The performer glances around again, and then disappears into the trees on the far side of the hut, heading in the same direction as everyone else did earlier.

You wait awhile longer and a faint breeze brushes your skin, tickling your nerves with that strange sense of the island breathing.

Finally, the warblers start singing again and you wander out of the wind and into the bamboo hut. It appears much the same as it did the last time you searched the place. Across the top of the bar, one of the picture frames lies in shambles with the canvas torn out. Allen must have taken the sketch of the island with him.

Since you didn't get the chance to before, you peek behind the bamboo bar to find tankards sitting upside down on a shelf below its surface.

Running a palm over the top, you find it's smooth but bumpy, the rind of the bamboo facing upward and making the surface uneven. Such a texture would be ideal to hide a hidden compartment. You knock on the top, sides, and bottom, and then press against the shelves to see if anything gives or sounds hollow but nothing seems out of the ordinary.

Skip to page 118 to continue.

There's a moment where you wonder *how* you're going to get Allen to leave without you, but he doesn't even glance back when he stomps out the door. A peek through the window confirms he's heading straight toward the beach with a bounce in his step and a whistle on his lips. He never checks to confirm you're following.

You wonder how long it'll take him to realize he's alone. Then it occurs to you he might come stomping back, angry at you for not following, which will shorten your time.

You sweep a look over the hut and head for the bar. It's a simple bamboo structure with tankards sitting upside down on a shelf below its surface.

You run your palm over the top, finding it's smooth but bumpy, the rind of the bamboo facing upward and making the surface uneven. Such a texture would be ideal to hide a hidden compartment. You knock on the top, sides, and bottom, and then press against the shelves to see if anything gives or sounds hollow, but nothing seems out of the ordinary.

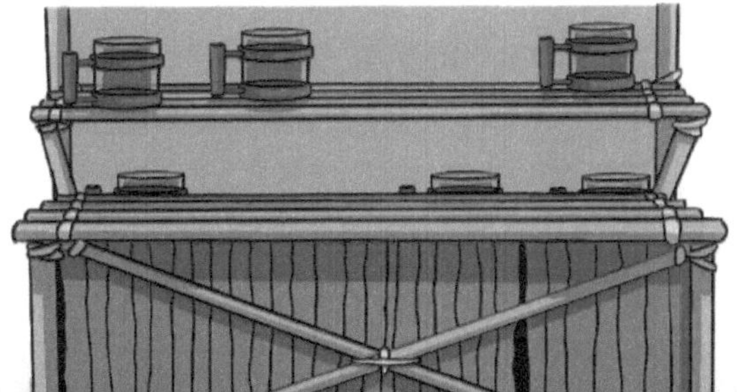

You quickly search the hut one more time before moving on to the trapdoor. A firm pull on the waterfall painting produces the click you heard before and this time a small notch appears near your feet, right where the wall and floor meet. You use it to pull a section of floor upward.

A gust of briny wind presses against your face when you peer down to find a wooden ladder leading into darkness. Judging by the wind, it's a tunnel. With a small grimace, because heading into a dark tunnel rarely leads to good things, you pull out your boot knife and descend the ladder.

It creaks abominably, echoing through the tunnel like a trumpet announcing your presence.

Once at the bottom, you pull the trapdoor closed by way of a rope hanging from the bamboo door above. It clicks into place and total darkness envelopes you. In the sudden stillness, your breath whispers out of your lips.

You shift away from the ladder and press tight to the wall, hoping you're not now in a goblin's den. The briny wind brushing your skin doesn't carry their usual stench, however, so you continue forward with your left hand against the tunnel.

A flash, bright and painful after the complete darkness, blinds you and the tingle of magic flares across your skin. You duck to the side, raising your knife as you do.

"Don't need that here," a voice rasps.

Blinking furiously, your vision finally clears. You're no longer in the tunnel. Instead, you stand in a cavern that's lit by the daylight filtering in through a small entrance to your left. Most of the cavern is occupied by a dark pool of shimmering water. Perhaps because it's an enclosed space, the tingling feel of magic seems particularly strong, making you shudder.

"Disorienting, isn't it, Hunter?" says the same raspy voice.

This time, you spot the speaker.

Patricia, the storyteller, gives you a mocking smile through her long dark hair. She sits against the cavern wall with her fingers trailing in the pool beside her.

"Yes," she says at your surprise, "I know you're a hunter." A fit of shaking doubles her over toward her knees. The motion seems odd, though, only affecting her torso and arms. Finally, she straightens back up with a weak groan.

"What happened?" you ask, putting your knife away and going to her.

"Thought the King's

hunters were smarter than that," she snickers. "You found a portal. According to myth, the island's riddled with them."

Although the information's useful, that wasn't what you meant. "What happened to you?" you clarify.

A bitter smile answers. "Got into something I shouldn't have."

"What was it?" you ask even though you suspect it's poison. If you can place where she ran into the substance, maybe you can pinpoint the poisoner.

"Don't rightly know," she says. "Could've been the rum I drank or the fruit I ate or even bad water. Started to feel the effects not long after the *King's Justice* dropped us off, so I headed here."

She sniggers at your questioning expression, but then another fit of shaking hits her and she clutches her stomach. Finally, she calms and leans against the wall again.

"I'm a storyteller, Hunter," she explains, "and there are marvelous stories about this island."

"What story led you here?"

"This is the least explored spot on the island, or so the stories claim. Figured it offered the best chance of finding a shell, but then—" She shrugs and flicks her fingers at her legs where they're stretched out in front of her.

You realize why her fits of shaking look so odd. Her legs sprawl on the floor, her bootheels dead weights leaving divots in the sand.

"Probably a fool's hope," you mutter, startled that the poison is paralyzing her. "No one's ever found the shells."

"Ah," Patricia says and points toward the pool. "Crouch low and look."

Curious, you do as she says. The water shimmers, almost iridescent, and the faint light filtering in through the cavern entrance glistens in the crystalline water all the way to the lake's bottom. It gilds a multitude of white, black, orange, and even red shells. There must be hundreds of them, you figure, a collage of chipped, whole, and halved carapaces. Then your eyes snag on one tiny golden speck.

"You see it," Patricia rasps, watching your face.

You move with the intention of stepping into the water and Patricia's hand shoots out, weakly grabbing your arm with the bejeweled fingers she had trailed in the water.

They're so cold you jerk in surprise.

"It's easy to see," she says, hanging on, "hard to *get*. Each shell has a protection beyond being difficult to find. I think this one's the cold but now I'll never know because I can't even *try* to get it." There's a bitter edge in her voice as her hand falls away.

"Is there a trick from your stories?" you ask. "A trick to surviving?"

She stares hard at you, searching for what, you're unsure. "I don't know why the King's Hand sent you here, but he must trust you." She bites her bottom lip and then recites, "*One sits, freezing, among its own kind. Drink deep, and of the cold, don't mind.*"

Drink deep? you ponder. *Well, there's only one thing to drink in the place.*

You cup your hands and dip them into the pool. Instant numbness locks your fingers into their cupped position and a shiver runs from your hands down to your toes and up to the roots of your hair. You gasp, fighting to draw the water to your lips.

Patricia stares, a mix of hope and shock in her gaze as you drink.

The water shoots ice through your teeth, and then it washes into your stomach and your body flushes with chills.

There's a familiar flash. Blinking hard, you find yourself surrounded by hundreds of colorful shells. Under your feet is a golden carapace.

It's as big as you are at the moment, but

you know from seeing it from above that it's no bigger than your thumbnail. Guessing your time is short, you lay down and span the shell's surface with your arms, grasping the edges with your fingertips.

When you do, another flash blinds you and you're kneeling, dripping on the edge of the pool with a tiny shell clasped between both palms. Another shiver shakes your body so violently you keel over onto your side next to Patricia.

The poison's progressed to the point that only her eyes shift to watch.

Finally, your body relaxes into mere trembling and you place the shell into Patricia's paralyzed open palm.

You both stare at it.

You're about to pick it back up and plop it in her mouth, not sure if she has to ingest it, when the shell disintegrates and Patricia's bejeweled fingers slowly curl around the resulting dust.

A long sigh escapes her and tears trail down her dirty face.

"I never would've helped you, Hunter," she admits in a whisper. "Why'd you risk it?"

"Should I have left you to die?" Shaking your head, you negate her need to answer. "Do your stories tell of the other shells?" you ask.

Suspicion narrows her eyes, but then she

frowns. "You don't want one for yourself, do you?"

You shake your head.

"I won't ask. If the Hand put you here, I probably don't want to know the details." Weakly, she points at the dark portal in the cavern wall where you entered. She recites, "*One lies, down and low, near the bed of drunkards. Come, neat each row, below the line of tankards.*" She shifts her finger to another dark hole in the cavern wall and continues, "*One falls, never landing, to the water clinging. Bring it down, bring it out, with the island singing.*"

"Two portals?"

She nods, waiting to see where you go.

To take the Tankards and Drunkards Portal, go to page 127
To take the Falling and Singing Portal, go to page 135

Jennifer M Zeiger

One lies, down and low, near the bed of drunkards. Come, neat each row, below the line of tankards.

You know exactly what tankards Patricia's riddle is talking about, so although you don't understand what the rest means, you head back through the portal to the bamboo hut.

You offered to take Patricia with you to search, but she laughed. "I'm no use to anyone yet," she said. "Send one of the Hand's men for me later."

So, you again stand in the tunnel below the hut, encased in darkness while you work to release the latch on the trapdoor. You run your fingers along the bamboo and strangle a cry when a nail slices your palm.

Muttering, you press a cloth to your injury and carefully trail your free hand around the outline of the door above you. Finally, a rounded nob near the hut's wall meets your fingers and, when you press it, it gives a familiar click.

Good so far, you think and push upward, relieved that the door opens. Something slides and clatters across the floor as you do. You pause, but when nothing else moves, you climb the wooden ladder to peek around the hut.

A mess of shattered glass and broken bamboo greets you. Dark pools of liquid soak into the shreds of painted canvas scattered about the floor. A moment later, the sharp burn of rum hits your nose. Maybe Allen came back angry or another contestant searched the place, but whoever it was, the person's not present now.

Is the glass from the tankards? You wonder, emerging from the tunnel and relatching the trapdoor. Once inside the hut, it smells even more strongly of rum. You cover your nose while shuffling glass and bits of frame back overtop the door.

Did the ransacker find anything?

It's possible. But when you think about it, you find it hard to believe anyone knows as much as Patricia about the island and its shells. Why would they? So, although the tankards lie shattered on the wooden floor, you doubt the ransacker connected them to one of the shell's hiding places.

Bolstered by this thought, you tiptoe through the shattered glass and spilled rum until you're standing behind the bar. The top shelves are empty, swept clean by whoever tossed the hut. But on the bottom shelf, near the back wall of the bar, sits a single row of tankards in a perfect line.

One lies, down and low, near the bed of drunkards.

Can it be? You think of the lake with its freezing, shrinking waters and the wind of the island that breathes magic across your skin. Is this any different? The island's magic permeates everything, and so why not have a row of tankards that always sits on the bottom shelf of the bar?

You kneel, careful not to press your knees into the shattered glass, and gaze into the bottom shelf. There's the clear glass tankards and the green and brown of the bamboo bar. No hint of gold, but then, the ransacker likely would have seen the shell if it were easy to spot.

Near the bed of drunkards.

You picture the last time you came across a drunk. It'd been an overweight goblin who'd plagued a town just outside the Alder forest. Tasked to take care of him, you'd found him sleeping draped over the edge of a horse's trough. He showed up the next day, passed out on the roof of a house and drooling on himself. You'd been called back a third, fourth, and fifth time, always finding him incapacitated in some awkward location until you finally relocated him across the country's border. He hadn't much cared where he slept.

Down and low…below the line of tankards.

You wince and proceed to lay on your back so you're looking at the shelf of tankards from below.

From here, you can see into each glass through the slates of the bamboo and, as you peer into each one, you find a tankard that doesn't have a glass bottom. Instead, there's a familiar array of white, black, orange, and red shells.

There's no hint of gold, but it's got to be in there somewhere.

Cautious not to move the tankard, you reach between the bamboo slates and slide your fingers into the mug. Instead of hitting the bottom, your hand keeps going and you feel a momentary flush of cold before you encounter the rough texture of shells.

If you take a handful, you'll end up with a monkey's fist problem where your knuckles will be too big to retreat out of the tankard portal. So instead, you slide shells between each of your fingers and withdraw your hand while it's still open.

The first group of shells is normal. So is the second. Then the third. You begin to collect a small pile beside you.

It's while you have your hand back in the tankard portal, your arm aching from the awkward position, that you hear boots thud against the hut's floor.

You freeze, holding your breath and

hoping whoever it is doesn't walk around the bar.

They do.

And you find yourself staring up into the lined face of Robert, the King's Hand.

He sighs, clearly relieved, and frowns at your awkward position.

"I was watching from the *Justice* and never saw you emerge after the performer left looking angry. It made me worry." He shrugs and cocks his head, looking at where your hand, wrist, and lower arm disappear into the too deep depths of a tankard. "What are you doing?"

Carefully, you withdraw your hand, fingers full of shells, and hold it out to show him.

You both can see the small golden carapace intermixed with the others and matching grins spread across your faces.

Robert finds you sitting against the wall outside the Queen's chambers, waiting to hear if the shell worked. With her so close to death by the time you returned, the physician expressed doubt that even a magical cure would help now.

From the relief in Robert's posture, the physician was wrong. He groans as he lowers himself to sit beside you, and then wrinkles his nose at the stench of rum wafting off your clothes.

"You need a bath."

"I'll get to it."

He nods, and you both stare at your feet where they're stretched out on the stone floor. It's a strange sight, your worn, dusty boots beside his polished black ones.

"I never value your work enough," he says softly. "Those shells have eluded us for years."

"You gave me the tools needed." You shrug.

"When I had the soldiers retrieve Patricia," he says, moving to another subject, "I had them search for the other four suspects as well. They're nowhere to be found."

Finally, you look over at him. "You want me to find them?"

"I do," he says. "One of them is still the poisoner."

You simply nod and push off the floor to stand.

"Oh, and think about what you'd like to do with Isbell Island," Robert says, surprising you.

"What?"

"You found a shell. The island's yours now."

What a disturbing thought. You shudder as you walk away.

The End

You find yourself standing in another dark tunnel having just experienced the now familiar flash of a portal. While your eyes adjust and the tingle of magic fades, you run Patricia's riddle over in your mind again.

One falls, never landing, to the water clinging. Bring it down, bring it out, with the island singing.

You shake your head, hoping *"bring it down, bring it out"* will become clear once you see where the portal took you.

A part of you worries for Patricia, who you left back in the cave, but she laughed when you suggested taking her along, saying, "I'm no use to anyone yet. Send one of the Hand's men for me later."

Now, a steady, damp breeze presses against your face while the tunnel is filled with the heavy roar of a waterfall somewhere ahead. You shiver from the now predictable tingle the breeze causes along your nerves, and sniff. A rank stench fills your nose but you can't quite place it amidst the smell of damp moss and water.

"It's not right, Uncle Nessen," shouts a high female voice over the roar of the falls.

The cook. She's the only other female on the island. Then you register her words. *Uncle Nessen?* That must be the scribe, which would explain why they started working together from the start of the challenge.

"What's he going to do with an island, Mia? He's three inches tall!"

You creep forward, trailing your fingers along the damp stone of the tunnel.

The argument pauses briefly before Mia says, "He's right, Uncle, there might be a way to return him to human size." And you realize someone else must have spoken but you missed the words over the roar of the water.

As you move closer, you make out two figures standing on a ledge of rock where the tunnel ends with a waterfall cascading behind them. The shorter of the two, Mia, is staring at her palm where she holds it out like she's having a conversation with it.

The other throws his arms up and starts to say, "Fine, but you're—"

"So tenderhearted of you," interrupts a new voice. You recognize it as Allen's, but there's a gloating sneer in his usually playful tone. "But it doesn't matter since I'll be taking that shell. I don't even have to resort to poison this time to get what I want."

He steps into sight, standing near the edge of the falls. He aims a crossbow at Mia while pointing with his free hand to indicate where he wants the girl to set the shell on the ground.

Pulling your knife, you're about to step forward and present your justice medallion when a high-pitched cackling fills the tunnel. Your stomach sinks and you finally place the rank odor. *Goblins.*

"Caught a passel of prey today!" hollers one, and there's the snap of tensioned rope being cut free in the tunnel behind you. It creaks and you look to see a log swinging sideways toward you. With resignation, you realize you walked right under their trap while watching Mia and Nessen.

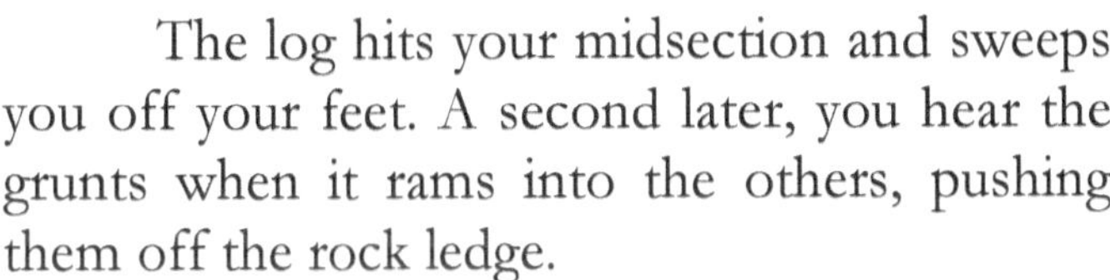

The log hits your midsection and sweeps you off your feet. A second later, you hear the grunts when it rams into the others, pushing them off the rock ledge.

Water slams into you, shoving you into the churning chaos below the falls. Your arm smacks into someone for a moment but then it's just swirling water and heavy pressure and the burn in your lungs. You're not sure when you let go of your knife, but it's gone, lost to the bottom of the lake.

You've never been under a giant waterfall before, but you have been in a churning river and you know to go limp so the water will spit you out farther downstream.

Forcing your body to relax, you realize

everything from your toes to the roots of your hair is tingling, but then an overwhelming desire to thrash for the surface hits you and you have to convince yourself to relax again.

Finally, the water spits you out several yards from the falls. As cool air brushes against your scalp, a thick, floating pine branch grazes your fingers. You grab ahold and are getting your bearings when Mia's dripping head appears nearby.

She flails, fighting the drag of her waterlogged skirt, and you push your branch into her hands. You can't stop glancing between her and the massive cliffs behind the falls, a sinking sensation hitting your stomach.

Mia notices and looks behind. Then she glances back at you and to the falls again.

"Oh no!" she says, "we've been shrunk like Marius Jack."

Shrunk. That's exactly it. Mia looks like a three-inch-tall praying mantis clinging to a stick compared to the waterfall behind her.

Just then, Nessen breaks the surface and flips onto his back, breathing hard.

"Oh, there's Uncle!" Mia exclaims as you direct the branch toward the scribe, who's also the size of a bug. "But where's Marius Jack?"

Nessen's head swings around. He spots you with Mia and glares. You see the wheels turning in his head as he tries to figure out where you came from.

Mia continues talking, still focused on Marius Jack. "We discovered him beneath the falls. He'd found a shell but he was only a pinch tall. Apparently, he fell into the river above the cliffs and washed over the waterfall. When he landed in the lake, it shrank him."

You remember Mia talking to her palm and realize it was Marius Jack she'd been speaking with.

Nessen grabs ahold of the branch, still glaring, but he doesn't have a chance to say anything before Marius Jack surfaces nearby.

"He doesn't have use of his legs," Mia points, spotting him as well. "Someone poisoned him and now he's paralyzed. That's why he fell in the river in the first place."

You see a flash of grayish-green movement behind the waterfall.

"Shh. Sound carries," you whisper while you swim for the dresser.

"Who—"

"Goblins," you mouth, pointing at the falls.

Nessen's protest goes silent.

Finally, you reach Marius Jack. He drapes his arms over the branch, pressing his forehead into the soggy bark in exhaustion.

Mia presses her lips tight and points to the lakeshore beside the cliffs. Allen, still human-sized, stands on the shore. He must have been close enough to the edge of the falls for the swinging log to miss him. Now he paces, scanning the lake.

On instinct, everyone sinks in the water, leaving barely their heads showing.

One blessing to being bug-sized, you figure.

Then you hear it, the same high-pitched cackling from before, and a moment later three long-armed, gray-skinned goblins amble out from behind the falls like misshapen apes. Their shoulders appear lumpy from carrying dozens of their tiny, shrunken brethren who hoot and holler in excitement.

The smaller goblins scramble down their companions' legs to the ground and start pushing small, leafy boats into the water while the larger three watch from the shore.

Somehow, they haven't seen Allen where he creeps back toward the trees.

"They're coming for us," Mia whispers.

These goblins are grayer than the mountain variety you've dealt with before, but you suspect they're not much different beyond that. And all goblins love a good ambush, hating it if even a single person escapes.

"Hey," you shout, wincing as your voice comes out mousy. Nessen hisses, surprised, and Mia cowers. Marius Jack just lifts his head from the branch to gaze bleary-eyed at you.

"Hey," you squeak again.

The goblins' long ears swivel and

the group in the boats begins chattering when they spot you.

"You missed one!" you shout, pointing at Allen, who's almost in the trees now. The goblins turn and Allen freezes.

It doesn't help. They spot him and a collective howling comes from the gray beasts. They row back to shore and swarm up to the shoulders of their larger companions, who are hopping back and forth, eager to chase the performer.

Allen takes off into the trees, making such a racket that you can hear him over the roaring waterfall and the howling of the goblins as they give chase.

After a moment, the racket fades until all that's left is the roar of the falls and the soft swishing of everyone's arms in the water.

"Quick thinking," Nessen says.

Marius Jack nods and flips his hand over on the branch, revealing a golden shell no bigger than a normal pinky nail. "Guess this is useless now, isn't it," he says.

You stare at the shell for a moment, an idea forming.

"Maybe not," you say. "Let me explain some things…" As you speak, you show everyone the King's justice medallion around your neck.

Although you're all now bug-sized, you might still succeed in getting the shell to the Queen if you work together. Holding onto that hope, you lay out your plan.

The End

Jennifer M Zeiger

A review of the day tells you that the majority of the group will head to the cliffs, not the cave. Patricia, the storyteller, is a mystery, but you didn't run into her heading to the cave before, so it's unlikely you will now. That leaves Allen as the only possible one to follow the same route as you.

Which means the cave is the least searched location. As you climb over the ship debris to head south again, you mull over the problem of the roc. Somehow, you'll have to get around it to reach the cave.

You step off a chunk of planking, sand squishing under your feet, and pause. Peeking out of the white sand is a bright red and blue shell. Not a seashell, but the hard surface of an enormous bird's egg.

A roc's egg.

It must have fallen through the portal at some point. Stepping closer, you feel heat radiating off of it and realize the baby roc might still be alive.

Before you know exactly what you're going to do with it, you're fashioning a carry sack out of ripped sailcloth from the debris and slinging the egg over your shoulder.

It's heavy, and hot, but you trudge your way through the tall grass and into the trees.

Without Allen rambling along beside you, you cross the island in half the time it took before, despite the extra weight of the roc's egg. Between the heat of the day and the egg on your back, you're covered in sweat when you reach the hill below the roc's nest.

The island's palms and pines fade away and you stare at the shale-covered hillside, studying it in hopes of finding a way to avoid passing so close to the dragon-sized bird.

With more time to study the terrain than you had the first time, you spot a jagged but larger cave entrance farther up the hillside above the nest. On either side of the hill are cliffs and you can barely hear the crash of the ocean's waves beating beyond. Unless you can climb those cliffs, you're not reaching the cave any other way than past the roc.

You creep forward, stepping carefully to keep the shale from sliding. Still, it grinds beneath your boots until you reach the lip overtop the nest.

You lay on your stomach to peek inside.

The giant bird sleeps in a massive nest built from broken masts, splintered planking, and even the curve of ships' hulls which are used to line the outside edges. The portal sits to your right in a swale, or natural ditch, leading from the nest to over the cliffs. In a heavy rainfall, debris would wash from the nest straight through the portal, and you suspect that's exactly what happened to the egg you now carry.

Bits of metal wink in the swale, reflecting the noonday light. Some echo the gray of steel, others the brownish-gold from brass, and then, almost in the nest, a different color catches your eye. A faint golden hue.

A shell.

It makes sense. The roc collects debris from all over the island. If someone found a shell and took it back to their ship, then it wrecked or the roc attacked, anything on the ship would end up in the nest below.

Your first inclination is to sneak down to take the shell, but getting caught by the roc, who has remarkable hearing, almost directly in the nest would be a death sentence.

The other option would be to attempt a trade with the egg you found, but you're not sure how smart rocs are. You've only had a few dealings with the giant birds, all of which involved running away, not talking. Will the bird understand the trade idea?

As you debate, you watch the rise and fall of the roc's steady breathing.

To sneak down to the shell, go to page 149
To trade the egg, go to page 155

Trying to trade with beasts has rarely gone well for you. So, you decide to sneak down, leave the egg at the edge of the nest, and steal the shell.

Snugging your improvised carry sack more securely on your back, you slowly begin to descend into the nest. The shale gives way to clear, sandy ground, which makes each step quieter and more stable as you move. Every few steps, you glance over to make sure the roc hasn't awoken.

By the time you reach the edge of the debris, its sides still rise and fall in steady rhythm. You skirt around, heading for the swale, and are almost to it when an echoing *crack* sounds behind you.

You freeze.

It's a moment before you realize the egg on your back is moving. You swing it to the ground. There's now a crack running from the top to almost halfway down the massive shell.

Something snaps in the nest and you look up. A huge golden eye glares back at you.

Quick as a snake, the roc's beak darts forward and snatches you around the waist. The move also pins the carry sack with the shuddering egg against your leg.

You scream as your world spins. You wait

for the bird to swallow you but instead it rears back and drops you…directly back into the time portal.

There's the now familiar flush of heat and flash of light and you tuck into a roll, hoping to avoid getting hit by the egg.

You're still blinded from the flash when you hit the sand. As you come to a stop and your vision clears, two things register.

The sun is exactly where it should be in the sky, and there's the call of birds, but instead of the warbler's familiar trilling, you hear a high pitched, "Watch it, watch it, watch it."

I didn't go back in time. You roll over with a groan, intending to see how the cracked egg fared.

The sound comes out scratchy and you frown. Everything feels—weird. Nothing hurts. Looking at yourself to take stock, you go very still.

You're not staring at your leather boots, but at huge claws and a belly covered in a soft down of red and blue feathers that create a deep purple when layered together.

It's then you notice there's no egg on the sand around you.

Crazy wild magic. Crazy portal.

Everything you had on you is gone…except for the King's justice medallion, which still hangs from its cord around your neck.

You dance around a bit, taking in the feel of your clawed feet and the pull of the long wings extending from your sides.

"Happy dance, happy dance, happy dance," says a voice.

You turn toward the tall grass of the dunes where a sandpiper dances sideways.

"Teach me to fly?" you ask.

It cocks its head. "Extend and flap, extend and flap."

An idea starts to form. Since the sandpiper and the warblers aren't scared of you, you may have some new allies.

Turns out, flying takes a lot more effort than simply extending your wings and flapping, but you eventually figure it out. And along the way, you make friends with the smaller birds and convince them to snag a certain shell from the roc's nest on the island.

Now, you fly toward Capital City and the King's palace with two things in your beak—a shell and the King's justice medallion.

The appearance of a giant roc will certainly cause a stir, but you plan to keep your visit brief. Inside, you feel a pull to go home, back to the Alder forest, that you're finding hard to ignore. According to the warblers, this is normal.

You scan the skyline and wing closer to the palace where it rises above the other buildings in the capital. You're searching for a familiar figure. Finally, when the sun peeks over the horizon, you spot Robert, the King's Hand, standing on the eastern parapet enjoying his morning coffee.

His mouth gapes open when he sees you and his fingers clench, frozen around the mug sitting in front of him on the parapet.

Winging onto the wall, you grip the stones in your claws and feel them give way slightly under the pressure. Thankfully you're not full grown yet or you might have crushed the tower's roof. Despite that, you wince, still not used to your new strength.

Robert's just now inching toward the stairs to escape but you lower your head to block the door and open your beak.

Your items ping against the floor and before he can react, you fly away. No need to stay longer and chance archers shooting at you. Besides, home is calling, pulling you back to the forest.

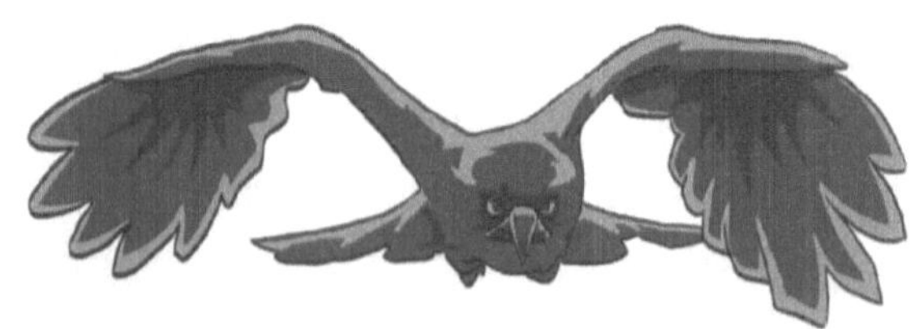

Robert holds the Hunter's justice medallion in his palm while he leans on top of the parapet wall. In his other hand he holds a letter containing news from the Alder forest.

He wondered at first when the roc delivered the shell if it'd eaten his friend, but now he smiles. According to the letter, a giant bird keeps frightening away trolls and bears, making the forest one of the safest places in the country.

Robert shakes his head. Isbell Island contains some of the most untamed magic he's ever encountered, and he doesn't even want to know how his hunter got turned into a giant bird, but he's glad the hunter's happy back in the Alder forest.

The End

Of all the majestic beasts you've encountered, rocs are the most solitary, only attacking when they feel threatened. You decide to attempt the less threatening of your options.

Standing at the edge of the nest, you cradle the warm egg in your arms and call, "Hello?"

The rhythmic breathing of the bird stills.

"I found something of yours," you say.

The roc's head lifts and twists to look over her shoulder. Like a dog's hackles, the feathers along her neck rise, making the already huge bird appear even bigger as she stands and turns.

You hold up the thirty-pound egg while fighting the nervous shake in your arms. The roc's head sways, her long, curved beak coming uncomfortably close to your nose.

"May I have the shell?" you ask.

The head tilts and you point with your chin toward the glittering carapace. But the bird simply goes back to studying the egg you hold. She shuffles backward and looks beneath her feet.

Inside the nest sit three similar blue and red mottled eggs. The roc taps each one, counting. She does it again before rearing up with a cry that makes your ears ring.

You realize the roc knows she laid three

eggs, and you're holding a fourth. She's not going to recognize the egg as her own because it's either from a different timeline or an earlier batch.

Or that's what you figure in the split second before the roc's beak darts forward, trying to skewer you. With a yelp, you dodge to the side but the weight of the egg makes you stumble.

It slips from your fingers, cracking against the ground. You cringe but don't have time to check on it before the roc darts at you again. You roll and the beak barely misses.

There's a resounding *crack*.

You finally get to your feet and duck under a chunk of ship's planking. Across the way, the egg rocks on the dirt with spidery cracks running its entire blue and red surface.

Then the planking above rips away, revealing you like an oyster in its shell. Claws scrape on metal while the roc tries to grab you and you scramble over timbers to duck under her massive wing, the long feathers brushing your back.

You need to get away or hide in the small cave you saw the first time you climbed the hill. Searching for the cave, your toe stabs into a rock and you hit your knees. There's a scraping behind you and you twist only to have giant claws slam into your chest, pinning you to the ground.

The roc screams in triumph and you cover your head with your arms, expecting her to finish you.

Something screeches in response, lacking the depth and volume of the larger bird, but still angry and demanding.

You peek through your arms. A baby roc stands beside you with its blue and red feathers still wet from the egg. Its head barely reaches the adult roc's belly, but it pecks at her claws where they pin you and screeches again.

The adult roc stares and then glances back at her nest to be sure her three eggs still sit inside unhatched. Reassured, she screams at the chick but the chick screeches right back.

Reluctantly, the adult removes her claws and steps away. Before relief can hit you, however, the bird spreads its massive wings and starts to flap, shoving you backward across the ground with a heavy wind.

The chick slides with you despite its efforts to dig its claws into the dirt. As you fight your way to your feet, the roc follows, chasing you farther and farther from her nest.

You hope she'll give up once you reach the bottom of the hill, but you soon realize she's going to follow you until you're off the island.

"Come on, Screech," you encourage the

chick while you help it waddle through the trees with the adult circling overhead. It can't fly yet and its walk looks like a duck's. "There's a boat to get us away from here."

You're not sure if the chick understands, but it sticks with you.

"Only you," Robert, the King's Hand, says, "would manage to befriend an infant roc."

The chick, who you've named Screech after his high-pitched cry, suns himself in the meadow beside the King's palace. After only a week, he's the size of an ox.

"Any luck on the island?" you ask, chaffing at having to give up your mission because of the angry adult bird.

"We found a portal into the cave you were trying to reach. Patricia had already gotten there but someone poisoned her, which paralyzed her. She was literally pointing at a shell there. We retrieved it but—" Robert winces.

"What?" you ask.

"The men are about this big now." He holds his fingers three inches apart. "We're not sure how to fix that but the shell saved the Queen and we reached Patricia before the poison killed her, so I've sent people back to search for another."

"And the others?" you ask while you pull out a chunk of meat from a crate on the ground.

Screech notices and climbs to his feet to investigate.

"Gone," Robert says. "We can't find any of them."

You pitch the meat into the air and the roc catches it, guzzling it down.

"So, no idea who the poisoner is?"

"No. But I think the danger's passed."

Silence falls for a bit and Screech wanders closer to investigate the meat crate at your feet. He's soon tearing it to pieces with his sharp beak to finish off the last morsels inside.

"I've got a new mission for you, if you're up to it," Robert finally says.

You scratch the side of Screech's head and nod, "What've you got?"

"There's a troll bothering the northern mountains…"

You agree to the mission, glad to have a partner as Screech follows you out.

The End

Acknowledgments

God has blessed me so much by the amazing people who help me with each book. I love this creative adventure and it's a joy to share it with others.

Like many, I struggle to ask for help. It's easy to fall into the lie that a book is all the author's, that every lovely word, every decision, every ending, comes from the author's mind alone. That is rarely the case and for me, never the case. And with *Golden Shells*, I needed a lot of brainstorming to weave together the various pathways.

So, to start, thank you to my Mom and Dad, who almost daily dealt with me showing up, saying, "So, if the Hunter's in this situation…?" or "Hey, I don't like this option, but what are some others that *fit* this world?" And without fail, they put aside whatever they were doing to spitball ideas.

Along with my parents are my beta readers. It's incredibly hard to hand over a story for feedback, but every single one of my beta readers brings something to the table and their feedback is invaluable. So, thank you to Mollie Bond, Leslie and Nick Rohman, Mom and Dad, and my wonderful husband, Nate.

Thank you also to my editor, Darren

Thornberry. I first got to work with Darren on *Discarded Dragons* and loved his enthusiasm for the story. He's patient with the multi-ending shenanigans and brought a polish to *Golden Shells* I never could have achieved.

Thank you as well to Justin Allen. Justin's worked with me on every single one of my books and for *Golden Shells*, the depth to his beautiful artwork just made sense. It helped tie this story together. Thank you, Justin, for all your amazing work.

Now, although I've thanked him already in the beta reading, I have to thank my husband, Nate, again. He sees the book process from start to finish and cheers me on every step of the way. He's my mental support, my IT support, my formatting support…this list could be endless and I can't thank him enough. I wouldn't be writing or producing books without him.

And last, but far from least, thank you, Readers, for giving my writing a chance. I love hearing how the Adventures are making a difference in encouraging young readers, and you make the work so worthwhile.

Other Books by Jennifer M Zeiger

Discarded Dragons

Not all dragons are created equal, as you well know. Some have wings intricately designed so their metal plates fold smoothly against their ribs. Others boast jeweled eyes that sparkle in the night. And still others possess needle-sharp claws that help them perch on the edges of shelves like birds of prey.

You are not one of these, however. You hide in a pile of discarded metal parts on the floor and watch the others through a single, murky glass eye. The Maker tossed you aside when he found your thin wings were too weak to carry your body.

The Maker's current project holds a lot of hope for you, though. She's small and many of the parts not deemed worthy of her perfect shape might fit you.

As night sets, you see your chance to sneak out and complete your design, to be a finished creation, but choose wisely, Dear Dragon, for success or failure depends on your next move.

The Adventure

The Adventure includes three different multi-ending Adventure stories, giving the reader 26 possible endings to find.

Moonrise Mountain: Legend tells of the wild horses that live atop Moonrise Mountain. Now you're out to discover if legend is true, but first, you have to reach the top of the mountain, and each choice you make will bring unforeseen dangers.

Temple of Night and Wind: Many have entered the Howling Maw in search of its treasures. None have returned. But now your village is starving and the Maw's treasures are your last resort. So down into the Maw you venture...

The Tournament: To free your uncle from life in the King's mines, you enter the Tournament. However, this is no typical contest, and its lack of rules makes success all the more difficult and defeat all the more deadly.

Pick wisely, Dear Reader, for success or failure depends on your choices.

Quaking Soul

This is it. This is Na'rina's chance to prove to her mother and the Dryad Council she can navigate the mythic and human worlds. With night hanging over the city, all she needs to do is sneak in unseen, attend a mythic meeting, and report back. If only she knew who had called the meeting in the first place.

Na'rina is a young Drydanda, destined to be Queen of the Dryads, or tree nymphs. Her world—fauns, nymphs, dwarves—hides in plain sight from the more populated human world. As long as they remain myth, they remain safe.

He's come to warn them but he's a wer-im, a werecat, who was banished centuries ago with the rest of his species for burning the dryad's trees. But humans captured his leader and dozens of other mythical creatures as well. If the mythic world is to survive, he must forge alliances.

When Na'rina's mother goes missing, she finds the violent, banished wer-im her only allies. She soon realizes that everything she's been taught about leadership appears to be wrong.

Who can Na'rina trust while attempting to keep the dryads alive in her mother's absence? As she quickly discovers, the fate of the mythical world rests on her decisions.

Jennifer M Zeiger grew up in the Rocky Mountains of Colorado and now lives in South Carolina with her husband, Nate.

She blogs multi-ending adventure stories and has now turned five of those into books—Three in *The Adventure*, and now two stand-alones, *Discarded Dragons* and *Mystery of the Golden Shells*. She also writes fantasy novels. Check out *Quaking Soul* for the first installment in the Hidden Mythics series.

jenniferzeiger.com

Note from Jennifer:

Hello Dear Reader,

Thank you so much for reading *Mystery of the Golden Shells!* I hope you enjoyed it. It is only because of people like you, people who give my writing a chance, that I'm able to do what I truly love.

If you enjoyed this book and would like to help, then please consider leaving a review on Amazon, Goodreads, or anywhere else readers visit. Word of mouth is a huge part of how well a book sells, so if you leave one, you are directly helping me continue this journey as a full-time writer. Thank you in advance to anyone who does. It means the world to me!

Many Blessings,

Jennifer

Amazon